A Matter Of Convenience

By Melisant Scott

A MATTER OF CONVENIENCE

Original © September 29, 2011 Melisant Scott;
reprinted © April 2, 2012 applies to revision and new
cover. OPEN WINDOW PUBLICATIONS, Texas, USA.
888.204.4144

Introduction

Darius McCoy a retired Army Colonel, decides its time he had a son. Jaded by a tragic marriage, he finds trusting women difficult. He yearns for a quiet life and his own ranch. The only problem was he would have to deal with a woman under foot. He preferred a docile woman. The luxury of time was not his. On a whim, Darius sends away for a mail order bride.

A short time later, an Eurasian, Moriah Kinsley who is born to a British father and Malaysian mother, looks forward to her new life with some trepidation. Once an affluent, well-educated woman, Moriah finds herself penniless. Time was of the essence, she boards the plane to begin her new life in America. On arrival, the two are joined in marriage and their new life begins. Moriah has a new country, culture and husband to deal with, but Darius baffles her most.

Darius and Moriah feel awkward in the new relationship. Darius finds it difficult to express his thoughts to a woman. Let alone, someone who has a say in his life. If only he didn't need a woman to have a son. Moriah strives to become the woman he wants. Darius will allow the relationship to progress just so far.

Moriah dislikes his motivation and yearns for a real marriage. He questions his ability to love. The hurt and distrust went deeper than he realized. But the emptiness in his life had taken its toll. He desperately wants a son. A period of adjustment follows and Moriah wonders if he really cares for her. Darius sorely tests all that Moriah holds dear. When he suggests a belated honeymoon, she refuses. At this point, Darius is convinced their relationship is, A Matter Of Convenience. When she becomes pregnant and leaves him, how might Darius convince Moriah that she's his heart's desire?

DEDICATION

I dedicate this book to my husband, who has been supportive and an inspiration in my efforts of writing. His encouragement helped me to write this novel about a mail order bride.

Melisant Scott

Melisant Scott

Melisant Scott

ACKNOWLEDGMENTS

My special thanks to the many book publishers of the romance genre such as Harlequin Romance, Mira, Random House, just to name a few which have provided hours of delightful contemporary romance reading which is my favorite, my husband, family and my delightful cats who love me no matter what, I wish to extend my gratitude.

Melisant Scott

 **CHAPTER 1**

Moriah Kinsley shifted in her seat, the flight was longer than any she had ever made. Now she was flying to the other side of the world. The rich American paid her way without blinking an eye. Everyone said she had been lucky and Moriah agreed. It was time to depart Malaysia in search of a new life. She disliked her position in life, however she was penniless. Her family's sudden demise and her twenty-eight years taught her life was unpredictable and could always be worse. Moriah was glad to be alive and was thankful for the opportunity to start her life over. Now she wanted to forget the terrible memories.

A year ago Moriah reflected she was clearing tables in a small inn. It had been a full day and her feet were killing her, in lieu of this she looked forward to soaking in a hot bath. Sensing a fervent gaze watched her every move, she turned. A stranger studied her for several moments before approaching.

"A man would pay a great deal in the States for a woman with your looks," the stranger said, lifting her chin in one hand as she shrugged from his grasp.

"Who are you? And what do you want from me?" Moriah managed.

"An enterprising man," the stranger remarked. "Let me explain."

She jerked herself back to the present, Moriah remembered she accepted the American's marriage proposal. His name was unusual she was powerless to recollect until Moriah opened her bag and withdrew his photograph, studying the lean aristocratic profile. His name was written on the back. Darius McCoy's thick sable hair was threaded with gray at the temples. Indeed he was a handsome man she thought. His eyes reflect a strong character. How would he regard her?

Several hours later a voice overhead woke Moriah, she shifted in the seat.

"We are approaching Houston. There will be no smoking and everyone please fasten your seat belts," a voice announced over the speaker system. The 747 glided easily onto the runway. Moriah was scheduled to change flights at Houston Intercontinental Airport. After an hour lay-over she boarded the plane for Austin.

A queasy sensation began in her stomach when the plane began its descent forty minutes later. Her black wavy locks fell in disarray as she clutched her midline. Darius McCoy paid five thousand for the marriage contract Moriah mused, she hoped he wouldn't be disappointed. Moriah stepped from the plane and walked tentatively toward the terminal. Her heart quickened and she could not believe her eyes. There he stood lean and tall on the tarmac, his thick sable hair blowing about his collar as he searched the crowd. When she moved closer she noticed the gray hair at his temples made Darius look distinguished. What would she say to him?

Darius's clenched palms were moist. Several people had by now departed the plane. Was this the correct flight? Alas he saw her. The photograph failed to display her real beauty, nor hint of the petite, five-foot frame. She resembled an exotic princess in the long, red sarong Darius thought moving in her direction.

2

"Moriah Kinsley?" Darius inquired with confidence, although he knew the answer. He would recognize her face anywhere.

She lifted her gaze. "Yes," she paused. "You must be Mr. McCoy?"

Uncertainty filled him as he offered his hand, smiling. "I'm Darius McCoy."

Moriah nodded demurely, accepting his hand as he offered to take her carry-on.

Whatever second thoughts he may have experienced were tossed aside. She was indeed a beauty, and he was lonely. He wanted a woman to share his life, but most of all he wanted a son. He assured himself he would learn to deal with whatever this new lifestyle entailed.

"We'll get the rest of your bags, then" he felt awkward unexpectedly.

"This is all I have," Moriah responded, her eyes cast downward. This proved to be more difficult than she imagined.

"Really?" Darius remarked thoughtfully. Focusing on the task at hand, he gestured. "This way, I have a car waiting." Surely he could do better he contemplated displeased with the lame dialogue.

Moriah wondered why he held her hand so tightly. As they proceeded briskly through the crowd, she deliberated what kind of man was he? This might be the biggest mistake of her life. She reviewed her options and the list was short. In any event, she would not allow herself to be dragged through the airport! Groaning her displeasure, she wailed, "You're hurting my arm!"

Stunned, he halted. Turning to her, Darius released his grip.

Moriah struggled to keep from frowning. His fingertips were imprinted on her wrist. She rubbed her right wrist and shot him a look that communicated she was both baffled and wary of his behavior.

Disquieted Darius supplied, "Forgive me. I was concerned with getting through the crowd. I had no idea." His face colored as he fumbled with his hands. The excuse sounded flimsy even to him. He failed to understand why he making a fool of himself. Moriah managed a half smile as he placed a hand to the small of her back, guiding her through the terminal now at a slower pace.

Outside the airport terminal, Darius led Moriah across the parking area to a black, 1953 Cadillac Eldorado convertible. After placing her carry-on in the back seat, he opened the door and assisted Moriah inside. Once behind the wheel, Darius turned to Moriah. "What do you think of her?" She must consider him a total clod after the scene in the terminal. This was not a good start, he thought. Moriah shot him a puzzled look.

"The car. Isn't she a beauty?" Darius smiled proudly as he stroked the padded interior with one hand. "It cost but it's worth it."

"She's beautiful," Moriah agreed.

Darius enjoyed the soft lilt of her voice. She's definitely female, he thought. He turned the ignition, checked the rear view mirror, and glanced over his shoulder before pulling from of the parking space. When the sunlight hit the chrome grips of the steering wheel, the flashes of light almost blinded Moriah and she averted her gaze.

The twelve o'clock traffic was fierce, he thought. "I have arranged a small ceremony," Darius said glancing in her direction.

She gave a faint smile in any event his eyes were fixed on the road hence he didn't notice. America was unlike Kuala Lumpur in appearance Moriah considered although she would do her best to fit into his world. Aside from the awkwardness at the airport, she was pleasantly surprised. Darius was dashing with warm brown eyes and long lashes. Moriah felt the attraction between them immediately. He's just a man she reminded herself but what a man! With great effort, Moriah dismissed her musings. He must have sensed the direction of her thoughts, he turned at that moment and shot her an appreciative smile. She blushed.

Minutes later, he exited the highway with a series of turns that delivered them in front of a small white cottage, *Forever Yours Wedding Chapel.* Darius had planned well he mused, the Malaysian lab he contacted sent the blood test results over in advance. This left him with one problem, the marriage license. He managed to persuade a local Justice of the Peace to grant them a license after explaining the circumstances.

Her gaze locked with his for a silent moment. Darius uncoiled his six-foot-five frame from behind the wheel and stepped out. Moriah was convinced he was a man who knew what he wanted and wasted no time obtaining it. He had a leashed vitality about him she considered as she watched him walk around the front of the car. His black Italian suit fit him in all the right places, boasting of an athletic frame. Moriah took a deep breath.

"Ready?" Darius asked taking her hand. He noticed her lashes swept her cheeks as she smiled demurely. He placed a possessive hand to the small of her back and directed her forward.

As they entranced the wedding chapel, an older, buxom woman greeted them with a broad smile. She introduced herself as the Justice of the Peace's wife, Martha. Her eyes were trained on Moriah now. "Congratulations. You must be the bride." Instantly Moriah felt at ease with Martha, she bobbed her head. Shifting her gaze to Darius, Martha said, "Your parents are in the first room to the right." She directed them to the appropriate corridor. Apprehensively, Moriah turned to Darius. He greeted her with a smile and lightly touched her arm, indicating he wanted her to move forward. Everything was happening so fast, Moriah thought falling in step alongside him.

Consequently, Darius ushered Moriah forward dreading the inevitable introduction to his parents. He remembered their reaction when he informed them of his decision to take a mail order bride. They were against the idea from the beginning. He should have married Julie Cunningham, the woman his parents approved, except he did not love her. Darius steeled himself and moved forward with his most ingratiating smile.

"Mom and Dad, I'd like you to meet, Moriah Kinsley," he said with bravado. "The woman I have chosen as my wife." Darius smiled, shifting his gaze to Moriah.

She knew he did not expect an answer, Moriah was nervous and hoped no one noticed.

Seth and Rebecca McCoy smiled as they moved closer.

"We're happy for both of you," Rebecca McCoy began.

Welcome to our family," Seth McCoy chimed. "I know this is sudden but -"

Martha, the Justice's wife appeared once more and Darius moved to whisper something in her ear. In turn, Martha's gaze slid to Moriah. "Come my dear, you must dress quickly."

Darius wondered why Moriah held a death grip of his hand. Releasing her hand he indicated that Moriah should follow Martha. A pang of regret gripped Moriah as she timidly followed Martha.

What was he thinking when he planned the ceremony? Darius reminded himself that he was concerned with following through before he backed out entirely. The realization of his actions rang crystal clear. He was nervous as hell. Had he done the right thing? This will pass he assured himself, it's merely a case of the jitters. He remembered his family's concern over his decision.

As if his mother sensed the direction of his thoughts, Rebecca McCoy queried, "How could you choose a wife by such unconventional means?"

"The boy's always known what he wants," Seth McCoy countered.

Darius was grateful for his father's support. He knew his parents lost hope of him ever remarrying. Alas he gained his composure and joined the others. Seth rose and approached as Darius entered the chapel.

"We're cutting it close," Seth remarked.

Perspiration beaded on Darius's forehead and upper lip and his pulse drummed in his ears. Why was it so hot in here? he wondered. Darius could barely hear his father's words.

Concern laced Seth's voice as he said, "Something wrong?"

Darius's voice sounded a million miles away. "No."

"You look green," Seth stated, hoping to lighten his son's mood. He recalled the same feeling washing over him before marrying Rebecca. Still Darius sat staring into space. Seth began to worry. Alas Darius clutched his father's shoulder. "Are you sure this is what you want?" Seth asked, his voice husky with emotion.

Moving to embrace his father, Darius nodded. "Yes, but I am nervous."

Moriah was tense there was no other word to describe it. She could easily dress herself, but Carrie, Rebecca and Martha took pleasure in the small task. Pleased with her reflection, Moriah whirled before the mirror. The old-fashioned white lace wedding dress, long train and small white flowers placed in her dark hair took her breath away.

"Darius is a lucky man," the women chimed in unison. "You're beautiful." They blinked in amazement at the abrupt response that followed.

"No! I am the fortunate one," Moriah responded.

"I wish I had your looks," Martha commented, shrugging her shoulders.

During the ceremony Rebecca cried, she had lost hope of Darius remarrying. Her gaze travelled to Moriah, who looked beautiful in her gown and her son proud and debonair. Perhaps the Mc Coys were wrong in their opposition she considered. Oh well, fiddley dee.

When the Justice of the Peace announced, "You may kiss the bride." Darius responded immediately by taking Moriah in his arms, he had waited for this moment. Maybe life did begin at forty-three?

Moriah's heart was in her throat. Anticipation welled within her bosom at the brief contact of their lips. His strong embrace and warm lips were masterful in their onslaught.

The reception afterward was small with a buffet table that offered a myriad of foods from brisket to sausage, a wide variety of vegetables, salad, baked potatoes, beans and casseroles. Everyone filled their dish with assorted foods, while others returned for seconds. The laughter and congratulations flowed as freely as the beer and champagne.

On the trip to the ranch occasionally Darius would steal a glimpse of Moriah, he couldn't believe she was his wife. An hour later he turned the automobile off the main highway onto a dirt road. The sign above the entrance read, *The Flying M Ranch*. The time of reckoning she thought, swallowing the lump in her throat. Moriah's gaze settled on the gray farmhouse surrounded by several trees and shrubs as the afternoon sun pierced the lattice roof over the porch. Cattle grazed freely in the yard. On the porch near the entrance of the farmhouse were two rocking chairs. A large clay pot of purple and white periwinkles sat on either side of the entrance. Moriah smiled, this was her new home.

Darius helped Moriah from the car. "It's nothing fancy," he commented, "but it's home, all 3000 square feet." Moriah stood for a moment gazing in awe, tentatively she moved forward. Darius lifted her into his arms and carried her across the threshold. "Welcome to your new home, Moriah," he said, before he lowered his head to claim her lips.

Moriah's heart soared, the kiss left her body pulsing in hope he would never stop. She raised her head and looked around the room as Darius lowered her to her feet. Moriah wasn't sure her rubbery legs would support her.

The house was a savory blend of frontier and contemporary design. The room's peach and golden hues complimented hardwood floors, ivory walls and oak beams overhead which provided a warmness inviting one to linger. The house was sweet with possibilities Moriah considered, just the same the walls were devoid of artwork. This she would remedy.

"It's amazing," Moriah said in disbelief. Her remark must have pleased him, he smiled. Darius led her into the kitchen where a butcher block table with six jade lights overhead were centered overhead. A configuration of metal pots and pans hung mid-air over the butcher block island. Sunlight peered through the skylights onto an organized workspace. Moriah was exhausted and could not suppress the yawn that escaped.

"How thoughtless of me," Darius began, his gaze assessing her. "You must be weary. I will show you the bedroom."

Another yawn escaped her. All Moriah wanted was a hot bath and to rest. She was worn out from the flight from Malaysia and the wedding. Darius noticed the dark circles under her eyes. If she knew how sweet and vulnerable she appeared at this moment he thought. He closed the bedroom door behind him as he left the room.

Darius released a deep sigh now that it was over! He could hear the occasional guttural sound of a cow or the trill of a bird. If his guess was on target she would sleep for hours. Darius loosened his tie, rolled his sleeves and crossed to the armoire, pouring himself a brandy. The glass in hand, he moved to open the French doors. A warm breeze wafted inside spilling hair over his eyes. Darius pushed the errant locks from view before lowering himself into a chair behind an oak desk. The green stucco walls and terracotta floors lent the house a quaint appearance he thought. He was pleased and at peace with the world.

His gaze swept beyond the French doors to a well-manicured lawn with generous foliage. The red blossoms against a lavender sky entranced him and his mind began to wander. He recalled how it all began. His trip to Austin and the several realtors he visited before he located the five-hundred-acre ranch of his dreams. The rental car allowed him the luxury to investigate the area before the purchase. He wanted everything to be perfect.

Darius discovered late in life he wanted a home and family. His need for a home base prompted Darius to answer a magazine ad. The publication advertised women from foreign countries. Oriental women had always intrigued Darius with their sideways glances, soft lilting voices and sinewy limbs. A part of him longed to place a woman on a pedestal, someone who placed children, home and loyalty first. A woman, who considered a career only after her desire for a family was attained. He yearned to trust a woman. It would take someone special. This was his motivation for a mail order bride.

~* * *~

CHAPTER 2

Darius reasoned that a Malaysian woman could learn his way of life. She would make a good mother and would be family oriented. He disliked that he selected a woman from a magazine. Darius tried dating several times but it never worked, not to mention it required to much time -- time he did not have. A couple of weeks after responding to the ad several photographs arrived with short biographies of each candidate. One of the photographs seemed to reach out to him. She was an Eurasian woman with creamy, flawless skin, and brown almost black eyes. Her shoulder length black hair and finely arched brows imparted a Dresden appearance. Her full, pouty, lips implored a man to derive pleasure from them. Darius knew she would be the one. She had an untamed look as her namesake, Moriah.

How fortuitous to find a beauty Darius considered, he couldn't believe his good fortune. He was pleased with his choices and cherished the idea of realizing his dream for a home and family. As an army Colonel Darius was anything but indecisive. Once he made a decision he never looked back.

Tonight was one of reflection. His thoughts shifted to the night of his retirement party. His friend and army buddy, Benjamin Willis arranged the party. He and Ben entered West Point at eighteen with a friendship that spanned twenty-nine years. Ben was more than a friend to Darius, he was a brother.

Darius was the serious one whereas, Ben's carefree attitude made Darius want to slug him at times. He would miss Ben. A comical smile spread on Darius's face, as he moved a hand to cup his chin. Leaning back in the chair he considered, Ben might have been promoted several times. But life was to be savored, Ben would say. In any event Ben endured no leave, KP and latrine duty in the early stage of his army career. Excluding this, Ben seemed none the worse for it.

His request for Lieutenant Benjamin Willis to serve as toastmaster for his retirement party violated military protocol. The army's protocol could be stuffed Darius mused, they had been through too much together. That night the Officer's Club was festive and the room filled with people. Darius was impressed with Ben's efforts, the place never looked better. Everyone tried to talk him out of retirement, but Darius refused. Twenty-five years was more than enough!

A deep sigh escaped him as he folded his arms behind his head. A year ago he wouldn't have considered the possibility of marriage. Especially after what happened twenty-one years ago. It began when Darius was twenty-two. At the time he thought he knew everything and was indestructible -- until he met Nancy! The divorce dramatically altered Darius's life. He was convinced women were not to be trusted. This had proven unwise in the past.

Several years after the divorce, Darius thwarted many a designing female. His hardened shell made it easy for him to distrust them. When he began to waver, the old hurt and humiliation would surface until Darius felt a familiar knot form in his stomach. Now he wanted to bury the pain and go on with his life. His domestic life would be managed in an orderly fashion. Darius attended to every detail with precision from ordering a bride to purchasing the ranch of his dreams. He had laid the groundwork. Moriah would bear him a son to carry on the proud name of Mc Coy.

Moriah set the carry-on the colonial four-poster bed and ran one hand along the indigo comforter. It promised softness and security, two things Moriah wanted desperately. This was her new home but Moriah found it difficult to believe she was actually here!

Poignantly, Moriah remembered Kisha saved her life. The bitter memories returned time and again and quickly she would dash them from her thoughts. Kisha would be proud of her.

She moved into the bathroom. A gilt-frame mirror greeted her against a background landscape of trees and rolling hills outside a large tinted window. White tile covered the lower half of the walls. She noticed antique gold fixtures and a scalloped marble basin as she drew her hair upon her head, disrobed and stepped into the warm, jasmine scented bath. Soaking in a hot bath would relieve her tension and weary muscles.

The thought Kisha, her dear friend brought forth a multitude of memories, some good, some bad. Moriah missed her aunts, uncles and grandparents. She had no contact with them in the past year for fear of her life and theirs. The painful isolation from her family was almost more than Moriah could bear. Her fear in Malaysia that her identity might be discovered, kcpt her lips sealed. Kisha's family tried their best to fill the void in her life, but it would never replace her own family. She was an outsider. Moriah shuddered to think what might have become of her without Kisha's friendship.

Much later, she dried herself and slipped into a blue silk gown. This was her wedding night. Uncertainty filled her, Moriah wanted to please Darius. Moriah leaned back on the pillows, to rest her eyes for a moment.

Gazing outside, Darius pushed a compact disc into the stereo. James Taylor's hits began to play in the background. It was good to be home he thought. He was convinced he made the right decision. He experienced emptiness in his life far too long. Time was a precious commodity, and his household would be run on schedule. The sixty-head of cattle, few horses and chickens would be a beginning. He would gradually add to the ranch in time. Here he would be free of politics and he could set the rules and rear his children in his fashion. A look of pure satisfaction spread on Darius's face.

The exotic woman he had taken as wife was the perfect choice. He would introduce her to ranch life. Darius knew the long flight from Malaysia and wedding had overwhelmed Moriah. Nevertheless he wasted no time with details once he made a decision. He would acquire watch dogs for the ranch. Darius moved a hand to his mouth, as a yawn escaped him. He glanced at his watch, ten-thirty. It was time to call it a night he thought. He pushed up from the chair and closed the French doors.

The bedroom had been quiet for hours. He opened the door and crossed the room. Darius stood for several moments, gazing at the Eurasian woman asleep in his bed -- his wife. When he drew the covers to Moriah's shoulders, she released a feeble moan. If Darius could see his face, he would not believe the warm protective expression on it.

~* * * *~

Sunlight streamed through the windows, Moriah squinted as she pushed onto her elbows, brushing the tousled hair from her face. The bed on the opposite side had not been slept. Where was Darius? she wondered. She swung her legs off the bed and padded to the bathroom.

After bathing, she dressed in a jade dress and glanced at her reflection in the mirror once more. Her black hair hung free about her shoulders. Except for the faint appearance of circles under her eyes she looked fine she thought shrugging her shoulders. Moments later she crossed the room, opening the door. The house was unbearably silent she thought moving in the direction of the kitchen.

The scent of bacon wafted in the air. When Moriah entered the room, she saw several pots and pans cluttered the workspace and table. Darius shifted his attention from the bowl he stirred to look up. A small towel hung from his tee-shirt clad shoulders. Moriah noticed when he moved each muscle was outlined in the faded jeans he wore, he wiped his hands on the towel. A slow smile spread across his face as their eyes met.

"Breakfast is almost ready. How do you like your eggs?"

"Scrambled," Moriah answered. "I should prepare your breakfast."

"Enjoy it while you can," Darius remarked with a smile. "Have a seat." He gestured with a sharp sideward movement of head. She looked disappointed.

Moriah walked to the end of the butcher's block island and took a stool. "I could set the table," she said, rising.

"Give me a hand carrying these things into the dining room," he remarked.

She nodded mutely. An abrupt thud startled Moriah, she turned toward the sound. Darius grinned as bread popped up in the toaster.

"I've been meaning to fix the thing," he chuckled. "It's noisy but it works." She shrugged and gave him a faint smile.

Moments later they were seated at the table. Darius knew she was nervous. When their eyes met even for a moment Moriah would shift her gaze to her plate. He wanted her to feel at ease.

"Dig in, it's not that bad." Darius lifted a fork with eggs to his mouth, his eyes were trained on Moriah.

She shot him an uncomfortable look. Restively she ate in silence. Darius completed the meal and pushed his plate aside. He opened the newspaper creating a barrier between them.

Occasionally he would sip his coffee and peer over the paper at her. Moriah neither smiled nor offered conversation, she sat there similar to a scared rabbit. This was proving to be awkward he thought.

Several moments later, Moriah stood. She could bear the silence no longer and began to clear the table. Perhaps the work would ease her tension. Moriah felt awkward in this stranger's home. If he noticed, he gave no indication. Moriah had loaded the dishwasher and flipped the switch when Darius entered the kitchen, his cup in hand. She couldn't think of anything to say except, "Care for more coffee?"

"No. But I would like to show you around the ranch. Do you have some jeans?"

"Yes."

"I'll meet you outside in ten minutes." Darius was pleased to see her look of relief and smile.

Moriah was delighted they would have something to bridge the silence between them. She left the room wondering was this his idea of a honeymoon? She smiled and shook her head in dismay. It would take great effort on her part to understand American culture.

Darius turned the ignition of the Land Cruiser and within moments they were moving along the dirt road away from the farmhouse. "We have 500 acres," he said proudly. "I'll show you the boundaries."

Moriah was uneasy under his scrutiny. "You must be wealthy," she replied.

"I think we are prepared for any eventuality."

"Have you lived here long?" Moriah questioned. He shook his head. She waited but no response or elaboration followed.

She observed the grassed, hill country enveloped by mountains with scattered trees and shrubs on their drive. They passed a rudimentary stone building open on both sides. Moriah saw bales of hay clustered alongside the road. He drove for what seemed forever to Moriah. Now and then he would stop to indicate points of interest.

The ranch needs work." Darius pointed to a fence in disrepair. "The previous owner retired because of health problems. I have hired a good man to help me. I will introduce you to him."

She gave him a faint smile. "What are my duties?"

Darius shot her a puzzled look. "Let's see, I prefer breakfast at six-thirty. We have chickens to feed. And of course you will run the house according to budget."

She gazed out the window. "By all means." He wants a housekeeper, not a wife -- the unflappable autocrat. His primary interest was the ranch. He might have acquired a wife with less effort. What made him choose her? Moriah wondered. She considered him attractive, though unapproachable.

Darius parked the Land Cruiser along a hilltop overlooking the valley below. "This is my favorite spot," he said, guiding her forward. "We own the land as far as you can see." He gestured with a wave of an upturned palm. He paused. "We'll do some riding later."

"It has an untouched beauty," Moriah agreed. They were acting as polite strangers. Didn't he want to get to know her? He spoke as if the ranch was his sole concern. He's an unusual man and she vowed to make him notice her as a woman. Seemingly he regarded her little more than a servant. Puzzled she studied him carefully.

As if sensing her intense gaze, he turned and they collided, her body flush with his solid frame. Tingles shivered up Moriah's spine and a lump caught in her throat as each nerve in her body jumped to attention. Male appraisal flashed in Darius's eyes briefly, then disappeared. Amazed by his self control, she waited.

Had he taken her in his arms and kissed her passionately, she would have been an eager participant.

Darius stood steadfast for several moments, gazing into her eyes. Instinctively he gripped her shoulders and his head began its descent. Instead of kissing her, Darius cleared his throat and uttered a shaky, low laugh.

Go ahead and kiss me! Moriah's heart cried.

Turning away, he spoke as if an afterthought. "We had better go."

Moriah was speechless. No one had ever regarded her with such indifference. Perplexed she followed behind him.

Darius maintained his distance the rest of the day. Although he explained his plans for the ranch, he did not inquire of her background nor mention their relationship. The return trip to the farmhouse was made in silence.

His behavior confused Moriah. Anxiety warred doubt moreover she wondered if Darius was a self-centered man. She was determined to make him a good wife, but this would be difficult.

Darius parked and turned off the ignition outside the combination barn and bunkhouse. Moriah followed his gesture to go inside the barn. As they entered the barn, a coarse voice greeted them.

"Boss." A rangy, leathered-skin man approached.

His dark, craggy features frightened Moriah. She gripped Darius's hand tightly. As he moved into the light, Moriah considered he must be a man in his late fifties.

"Jason, this is my wife, Moriah McCoy," Darius began. "Moriah, Jason Harper, our ranch hand."

Pleased to meet you, Mrs. Mc Coy," Jason said removing his hat.

"My pleasure." Moriah gave Jason a modified nod.

"Jason will tend the stock and help with general repairs and upkeep."

"Boss, what do you want to do with Daisy?" Jason asked.

"Daisy?"

"The heifer with calf." Jason's eyes widened, his brows furrowed.

"Is she about to give birth?"

" Yep, boss. Afraid so."

"Separate her from the rest and make her comfortable," Darius began. "Will you handle it, Jason?"

"I'll holler if need be," Jason responded. "Suspect it won't be long now." His gaze shifted to Moriah. "Imagine we'll soon have a lot of young ones running around here." He glanced down to his weathered boots. Moriah's face colored. Darius smiled and nudged her toward the door.

Jason inclined his head. "Ma'am."

Grinning, Moriah glanced over her shoulder to Jason. She liked him instantly. He was gruff, but straight forward. Minutes later Darius parked the Land Cruiser outside the large farmhouse. Weary after the outing, Moriah looked forward to a hot bath. She enjoyed touring the ranch today with Darius. The trip was a pleasant distraction, something both needed. She suspected he was equally nervous. No doubt Darius was proud of the ranch. She anticipated the evening would allow them ample time to become acquainted. Moriah was anxious to learn more about her husband.

Darius glanced at his watch, four o'clock. "I'm sure you'd like to clean up after the trip. Let's take a bath?" he suggested with a grin.

"Sounds wonderful," Moriah managed in a squeaky voice. Did he mean it the way it sounded? He was her husband, she reminded herself. She crossed the room toward the bedroom. She realized with a start, Darius did not follow suit. Grateful for the respite she entered the bathroom, grabbed the shampoo, and stepped into the shower.

~* * * *~

 **CHAPTER 3**

Thirty minutes later Moriah entered the living room. An empty glass rested on a nearby table. She could hear the shower in the other room. Apparently her husband was equally modest. Smiling to herself, she poured a glass of the lush red wine. She leaned back on the wicker sofa with an appreciative moan and lifted the glass to her lips.

Darius joined her fifteen minutes later, his moist hair combed off his brows. She liked the way his navy western shirt tapered to a thin waist and flat abdomen above the black slacks he wore. Suddenly Moriah's heart beat a primal rhythm. Today Darius acted the part of a true gentleman. In any event Moriah ached for him to throw her over his shoulder and carry her to bed. Her mother would be aghast of her present thoughts she smiled. True he was her husband, but a stranger nevertheless. She would coax him into talking about himself. This would afford her insight into the man she had married.

He pushed a disc into the stereo, crossed the room and seated himself on the sofa, pouring himself a glass of wine. Soft jazz filled the room. Awkward was a mild descriptor of the way Darius felt. Her expression similar to Mona Lisa's, invited one, promising untold pleasures. Why was he holding back? Darius could lose himself in her eyes. He wanted to throw his arms around her and kiss her senseless. Don't act like an animal he told himself. Instead be patient. Everything has happened swiftly give the relationship time Darius thought. First he would gain her trust and respect.

She thought Darius appeared tense. Restless under his scrutiny, she took the initiative. She stood and began to massage his shoulders and neck.

He heaved a sigh of satisfaction, turning to allow her better access. He closed his eyes, savoring the sensation. Darius was convinced she held magic in her fingertips. It was good to be touched.

"Release all the tension," Moriah encouraged, as she massaged his back.

He could feel his body relaxing. "You're good at this," he muttered. "Have you had much practice?"

"Enough," Moriah evaded, stroking his lean, hard muscles.

Old suspicions rose to the surface, Darius held himself rigid. Women were innate when it came to their feminine wiles. Nancy had been. His sideways glance spoke volumes as he withdrew. He leaned forward and reached for his glass. "Tell me about yourself?"

She noticed his expression had changed. She wasn't sure she wanted to answer any of his questions. Especially if his posture was any indication of his mood.

"Where should I begin?"

"What made you decide to ..." He hesitated. No sooner had the words escaped him, Darius regretted the tone of his voice.

"To be a mail order bride?" Moriah supplied, her eyes engaging his.

Darius nodded. On the edge of his seat, he felt as though he waited for an axe to fall.

"You have a right to know," she began. Darius gave a faint smile. "My father was British and he took a Malaysian wife. Nevertheless he was greedy and became involved with the black market. Suffice to say, he made powerful enemies. Our house was burned to the ground one night while my family slept." Her voice trailed off. "Everyone perished in the fire."

"I'm sorry," Darius replied softly.

"I have learned to deal with it." Moriah lifted her chin, unaware of the pain in her eyes. "That was a year ago."

He admired her spirit. Moriah was a survivor he considered as his mind pushed forward. "Dance with me?" Darius lifted his brows expectantly.

Disconsolately Moriah moved into his arms. Darius gasped as the muscles in his stomach clenched. Moriah buried her face in his chest. Their left hands interlaced, his right hand moved to the small of her back securing her to him. She felt good in his embrace he thought. Darius held his breath momentarily.

"Why did you wait to marry?" Moriah asked timidly.

Absently he stroked her hair. "I've had my career. I'm retired from the army."

"And now you want a family?" she questioned. Her cheek rested against his chest. Moriah could hear the drum beat of his heart.

"A man needs a son." He cupped the crown of her head, drawing her closer than necessary.

Moriah winced. This wasn't the answer she expected.

A loud knock at the door captured their attention. Setting her from him, Darius turned and crossed the room.

"Boss, I need your help. The calf is coming breech," Jason said hurriedly, turning to depart. Darius strode outside without a word.

Disappointed, Moriah moved into the kitchen to prepare dinner. She hoped he would be attracted to her, however Darius realized a woman was necessary to provide him a son. He might have chosen an American. Surely a virile man like Darius could have his pick of women?

Still no sign of her husband two hours later, Moriah resigned to the situation at hand began to eat alone. She found it difficult to understand why Darius would reach out to her and when she responded, he withdrew into himself.

* * * *

Lifting her head from the pillow, Moriah thought she heard voices. The sound emanated from the kitchen. She recognized Darius's voice, the other was unfamiliar. Curiosity blossomed within her, she dressed quickly and opened the bedroom door.

Entering the kitchen, Moriah could see her husband sitting opposite a sandy-haired man. Darius looked up as she entered the room. When the stranger laughed the sound rumbled in his chest before it thundered to the surface. He slapped his thigh as he whirled to face Moriah.

"Lamar, this is my wife, Moriah." She moved to Darius's side.

Lamar rose from his straddled position on the stool. She was amazed how easily he moved for a man his size. He extended a meaty hand to her. "Ma'am."

"Moriah, this is Lamar Johnson. He owns the neighboring ranch," Darius explained.

"How nice of you to call." Reluctantly she accepted his hand.

"The wife and I wanted to welcome the new neighbors."

"Thank you. Did you wife accompany you?" Moriah questioned.

"Nora sent some of her homemade bread and a bottle of merlot," Lamar replied. "She said she'd drop by later." He gestured to items sitting on the countertop.

Moriah's eyes followed the direction of his gesture. "How kind."

Darius rose after several moments of silence. "Coffee anyone?" Moriah motioned for him to take a seat. She took his cup and walked to the coffeemaker and filled it and one for herself. After placing the cup on the counter top, she lowered herself on a stool next to her husband.

"Lamar, you mentioned you played football?" Darius asked.

"That's right."

"What position did you play?"

"Linebacker."

"Who did you play for?" Darius queried.

"Texas A & M." Lamar laughed and shook his head.

"Were you any good?"

"Yes. I played when we were unable to beat University of Texas. They were a good team in those days," Lamar began. "As a matter of fact, I am still teased."

"Why?" Darius inquired.

"I'm an Aggie and this is Texas country. I've heard every Aggie joke," Lamar said, "If you folks need anything, don't hesitate to give us a call. Our number's in the book." Lamar rose and moved toward the door.

Darius shook Lamar's hand. "Thanks for dropping by and for the house-warming gifts. Give your wife our best. We look forward to meeting her."

"My pleasure." Lamar said, smiling. "You'll find the ranchers in the area pull together. I enjoyed the visit. I must go." Darius and Moriah accompanied their guest to the door.

"People are friendly here," Darius commented. Moriah shrugged in a helpless gesture. "He knocked on the door and acted as though he was expected," he added.

Gazing around the kitchen with a puzzled expression," Moriah said. "You must be hungry."

Darius nodded. "Sure."

"But we have no rice."

"What?" he questioned incredulously.

"Rice. And I did not see fish or vegetables to prepare ulam."

"U-u what?" He laughed.

"Ulam. It is a way of eating raw vegetables with rice and prawn chili paste."

He chuckled. "On purpose?"

Moriah shot him a look of disapproval. "Green beans, leaves, creepers, green nuts and cabbage are suitable," Moriah continued. "We must attend to this."

"Make a list of what you need," Darius offered. She was serious about this! "Today I planned a trip to Austin and I thought we might do some shopping."

Her expression was serious. "But it is far away," she insisted. He gave her a sidelong look for a moment. She waited, searching his face. "I will make the list," she said quietly.

Darius frowned and left the room. He had not considered she would try to change his eating habits, though he might even enjoy it. Darius suspected this quiet woman might influence him beyond his fancy. He should check the supplies in the barn and moved purposefully in that direction.

Why did she make a production about vegetables? Heck he would plant her a garden. Perhaps Malaysians were an agrarian people? Darius laughed. There were distinctive differences between them. Maybe this wasn't a good idea? Half the time he considered Moriah ate like a rabbit. A man couldn't survive on vegetables alone.

Darius's doubts were often difficult for him to overcome. His divorce from Nancy though not visible on the surface left scars that inevitably caused him discord. His tragic marriage left a bad taste in his mouth to the extent he'd sworn off any relationship in the past. The hard-pressed fear of being at emotional risk with a woman still troubled Darius. In the past he travelled extensively for his career and the isolation had spared him of entanglements. Nevertheless the emptiness that filled him and his restlessness had taken their toll. The myriad of emotions plagued him for three years. Until six months ago, the army had fulfilled him.

Straddling a stool in the barn Darius remembered Nancy was beautiful when he married her. She came from one of the best families just the same she had strived unabashedly to change him.

Regardless how trite the issue, she was determined to have her way at all costs, whining and complaining when she met resistance. He vowed this would not happen again. Memories were necessary but it was time to plan for the future Darius told himself. He had accumulated a nest-egg in the military and paid cash for the 500 acres and large farmhouse. He planned this change of lifestyle as strategically as he planned any maneuvers in the service.

Darius stretched his legs and stood. He positioned the gray Stetson on his head and went in search of Moriah. As he strode toward the farmhouse he considered he would allow her to introduce new foods but he was determined she would learn to prepare his favorite dishes. When he entered the kitchen Moriah's petite frame was bent exposing her derriere as she searched the cabinet. His hormones swung into overdrive, Darius exhaled sharply. He turned on his heel and strode purposefully into the living room. Heaving a sigh, he could not believe the way he over reacted. He was convinced he had been celibate to long.

"Darius?" Moriah called, entering the living room. He was leaning against the wall, his eyes closed. "The list is complete."

He shook his head and pushed to stand.

"You're not ill?"

Darius shook his head. "Just waiting for you."

She gave him a puzzled look. "I am ready."

"After you," he replied in a strangled voice.

She preceded him through the door. Her jasmine scent titillated his senses. Moriah resembles an exotic rare flower he thought beautiful and redolent. Her black hair was mussed and her eyes sparkled with amusement. When she smiled several fantasies crossed Darius's mind.

Why the odd expression on his face? she pondered. She would never understand American men. His eyes said one thing, his lips another. The mixed signals confused her.

Resisting temptation Darius allowed her to climb unassisted into the Land Cruiser. She squirmed in the seat looking for the seat belt. Her movements were sensual. Or was this his imagination? He remembered how strained his jeans became when he found her bent over in the kitchen.

Moriah stared out the passenger window as the vehicle moved toward the highway. Darius looked as if he was deliberating something of importance she thought. She tried several times to draw Darius into a conversation. To her dismay, the trip was made in silence.

Darius parked the Land Cruiser outside a boutique, and he turned to her. "Ready?"

"This is not the market," Moriah chided softly.

"You're right. Get out." She followed his direction.

"May I help you?" an articulate saleswoman asked as they stepped inside the trendy shop.

"My wife needs help with a new wardrobe," Darius responded. "The works."

"What exactly are you looking for?"

"Everything from dress to work clothes," he responded.

"Work?" the saleswoman repeated.

"We live on a ranch. Moriah will need some dressy," he said, waving a hand in exasperation.

"Follow me," the saleswoman added.

"I-I," Moriah stammered.

"Nonsense. Go with her," Darius interjected. His tone brooked no argument.

"We have some lovely things that will fit you perfectly," the saleswoman supplied, smiling as she led the way.

Glancing over her shoulder to Darius, Moriah followed the saleswoman through the boutique. He never failed to bewilder her. Did she not please him?

The saleswoman gathered several blouses, jeans and dresses as she moved through the aisles. It would take Moriah forever to try the garments for size. The garrulous woman astounded Moriah. American women are peculiar she thought they were outspoken and unconcerned should their clothing brush a stranger in passing. This was unbelievable!

~* * * *~

 **CHAPTER 4**

Moriah was shown to a dressing room while the saleswoman hung several garments on hooks and hurried away, saying something Moriah could not make out. Several minutes later the saleswoman returned. "Your husband had an errand to run. He said you should take time in your selection." She peered over the dressing cubicle at Moriah. "How's it coming?"

"Fine." Moriah paused to look up. "Did he mention when he would return?"

"An hour," the saleswoman replied, walking away.

He caught Moriah off guard Darius considered as he pulled out of the parking space. She had no idea he planned for them to shop for her a wardrobe. Ranch life required jeans and work shirts, not the silky garments she wore. His responsibility was to see she dressed properly. Experience taught him that sometimes women could take forever to shop. This would allow him ample time for a quick stop at the pet shop.

He was eager for a time when they no longer felt awkward with one another. Darius wondered how they might warm to one another. Haul her off to bed! That would certainly do it, he chuckled. Just the same he would implement a less drastic measure.

Darius drove past the pet shop several times of late, however he hadn't stopped to go inside. He had grown up with a variety of animals in the house. Despite being a military brat, Darius always had a dog. Due to his father's frequent change in orders, Darius learned to quickly adapt to new surroundings. Now it was time for a real home.

Seth McCoy, a retired general had finally become a homebody. It was a shame his father had not decided this earlier. He might have enjoyed knowing his children while they grew up. In any event he was pleased his parents had settled down. His father's arthritis gave them cause to move to Arizona. He claimed the heat was much better for his achy joints. His parents purchased a home near their daughter, Carrie. Their grandson, Chris, saw more of Seth than Darius ever had. He had no regrets Darius told himself, the military supplied the discipline he needed. It allowed him to travel and see the world. It was unusual the way in which childhood memories crept into his thoughts. He smiled to himself.

"May I help you?" a young woman greeted as Darius entered the *Love Your Pet Shop*. The manner in which she watched Darius made him uneasy. Perhaps he had something on his face? Then it occurred to him, she found him attractive. He gave her an engaging smile.

"What kind of pet interests you?"

"Dogs." Darius looked thoughtfully around the shop. I prefer a Springer Spaniel."

"More than one?"

"And an English sheep dog."

"I think we can help you." She led him to the back of the shop. "We have some puppies I think you'll appreciate. They just arrived."

A beige and white English sheep dog caught his eye. The runt-of-the-litter won his heart instantly. "This one." Darius lifted the furry bundle to his chest, nuzzling it. The young woman smiled approvingly.

"The spaniels are over there," she pointed to an enclosed area along an adjacent wall. Six Springer Spaniel pups of different colors romped and tumbled playfully. Securing the English sheep pup next to him, Darius hunkered next to the Springer Spaniel pups.

"Well fella, which do you prefer as a playmate? He spoke to the pup he held in his arms. The puppy released an impudent whine. "Okay, okay."

"It's feeding time, I'll take him back. Take your time and look around," the young woman encouraged with a flirtatious grin.

He was pleased a younger woman found him attractive he thought briefly before shifting his attention to the puppies. Darius studied each pup as he lifted them individually from the pen. He felt like a boy once again. Each pup burrowed close, nudging Darius with a cold nose. Ultimately he chose a black and white spaniel. The problem was he liked them all.

"I'd like to pick them up in the morning. My wife and I have plans this afternoon."

"That's no problem," she assured him. He paid for the pups and left.

An hour and half passed since he left Moriah at the boutique. Darius became involved with the pups that he forgot the time. A bell tinkled overhead announcing his arrival as Darius opened the boutique's door.

"Mr. Mc Coy," the saleswoman said, "your wife is almost finished. I think you will approve of her choices."

With a curt nod of his head, Darius took a seat near one of the displays.

Moments later Moriah joined them. She wore a yellow dress with brown dots, cinched with a wide brown belt at the waist and brown pumps. A bright yellow ribbon tied her hair atop her head, and she was more than pleased. "Is it awesome?" Moriah asked, laughter laced her voice. She whirled before him.

Her enthusiasm was contagious, Darius gave a broad smile. "Awesome."

"I cannot decide which," she explained, deliberating.

He was soon caught up in her excitement. Moriah intrigued and exhilarated him all at the same time. Darius tilted his head to each side in appraisal.

"Well?" Moriah prodded.

Darius slid his gaze to the saleswoman. "We'll take it."

Moriah squealed in amazement. Darius couldn't suppress the laughter as he moved to her side.

"I want to wear this one," Moriah added.

After the saleswoman quoted an outrageous sum, Darius handed her a gold card. While she completed the transaction, his eyes shifted to Moriah. "It's done."

Her husband was a generous man she thought watching him gather the packages, then direct her toward the door.

Once they were inside the Land Cruiser, she threw her arms around his neck, kissing his cheek. "Thank you, Darius." He leaned into her embrace.

Slowly he moved his arms around her waist. What a heck of a time for bucket seats, Darius thought. Her hands moved freely through his thick sable hair. The muscles of his abdomen tightened as his lips settled over hers.

Without delay little tingles became major tingles in Moriah. Darius released a low groan in his throat, his tongue circled her lips before the imminent invasion. Moriah realized with a start that she was making a fool of herself in public. She was caught off guard by the desire she saw in his eyes as she withdrew. Since her arrival everything had happened swiftly she reasoned. Possibly Darius would forgive her disgraceful display?

He released a tortured groan and straightened his posture. This woman would be the death of him! Darius noticed a small crowd of spectators outside the Land Cruiser. He started the engine.

"Aw, how sweet," said one woman, who was a spectator outside their vehicle.

"This is better than the movies," commented another.

"I don't believe this," Darius snapped.

Moriah moved down in the bucket seat. She had humiliated him. This was unforgiveable.

The Land Cruiser jerked in its backward movement from the parking space then lurched forward tires squealing as they contacted the pavement. The vehicle slowed only after several miles separated them from the boutique.

"I thought you might enjoy dinner out?" Darius offered tentatively.

"That would be most gracious." Moriah gazed expectantly at him.

"What kind of food do you like?"

She moved her hand to chin thoughtfully. "I have always wanted to try Mexican." Moriah glanced up as if she expected to be chastised.

"Mexican food it is."

America is a wonderful place. Just ask for something Moriah thought, and it was yours. She was fortunate beyond her wildest dreams.

Minutes later they pulled into the parking area of a large restaurant, *The Sombrero*, a massive tan stucco building. After a brief wait they were shown to a table. When the waitress appeared at the table, Darius ordered for them.

The restaurant was dim inside except for the flickering candlelight in colored containers on each table. There was a Mariachi band clad in black pants, short festive jackets and colorful sombreros. Melancholy music wafted in the air as they drifted from one table to another singing. Moments later the waitress returned with tall, slushy drinks with an orange slice, for each of them. In addition, she served chips and salsa with the drinks and left.

"What is it?" Moriah asked, gazing at the drink.

"Strawberry daiquiri."

"It's been a wonderful day," Moriah exclaimed. "Americans have much to be thankful for."

"We tend to forget this," Darius murmured to himself.

"Did you say something?"

He shook his head.

Moriah's hand covered his on the table. "Tell me about your life in America?"

An enigmatic expression worked on his face. "There's not much to tell," Darius dismissed.

"America has many opportunities. You must tell me everything." Sincerity gleamed in Moriah's eyes.

Straightway the waitress returned interrupting the slow, easy conversation. She served each a large platter of food. Darius drew a cloth napkin into his lap. Moriah followed his lead and shifted her gaze to the waitress, who remained at the table.

"Care for another drink?" the waitress asked. Darius ordered an additional round.

"Oh my," Moriah exclaimed, pointing with a fork to her plate. She managed after an initial taste, "What do you call it?"

"Chicken fajitas," Darius mused.

"They must be," she said, considering. "Evil. They must be taboo."

"Taboo?"

"Ah, bad luck."

Darius's mouth spread in a slow easy grin as he gave her a sidelong look. "Only for the chicken."

Moriah discovered she had a weakness for chicken fajitas, Spanish rice and tacos. Each culture has its own culinary delights. She sensed her education had just begun. After a second daiquiri, Moriah was more than a little tipsy. Her husband enjoyed watching her, or so she thought. "Were you born in Austin?" she asked, relishing the new food and drink.

"Actually I was born in North Carolina," Darius responded. The second drink mellowed his reserve. "I'm a military brat. I followed in my father's footsteps -- attended West Point then, joined the Army. I'm retired after twenty-five years."

"Is this your first marriage?"

A reserved mask fell into place. "No."

Did she say something wrong? Everything thus far had fared well she considered. Moriah knew from the look on his face the subject should be tread lightly. Forging ahead she said, "What was she like? Your first wife?"

He heaved a sigh before answering. "Nancy was beautiful and from a family most men only dream of marrying into," Darius began. "We were wrong for one another. She needed someone she could bend to her will. She filed for divorce after a year claiming irreconcilable differences."

Moriah forced back a distasteful remark. The woman must have been a fool. She decided his unwillingness to speak of Nancy meant, it was a painful memory. Darius's account of the relationship sounded similar to that of a spectator. Moriah was threatened by this. It was not as if she was insecure as a woman. She knew men found her appealing. For the first time in her life, Moriah was jealous. Darius was bigger than life she considered, his engaging smile adds to his animal magnetism. His wary attitude piqued her curiosity. "How long have you been divorced?"

"Twenty years," Darius murmured, tracing the rim of his glass with one finger. He studied it as though he expected it to reveal a magnanimous revelation. "You?"

"This is my first."

Surprise and curiosity warred within Darius. His eyes searched hers, assessing. Yes, she had the look of inexperience and lack of confidence about her. "Tell me about your childhood," he coaxed, attempting to change the subject.

"I grew up the oldest of four children in Kuala Lumpur. It is the capital of Malaysia."

"What kind of work was your father involved in?"

"Tin mining."

"And your mother?"

"A homemaker."

"How is it you never married?"

"My father had money and I was educated."

"Education precludes the need for marriage?" Darius leaned back in the chair. Before she could respond, he continued, "What were you trained in?"

Uncertainty filled her as she spoke. "I was an interpreter for a trading company in Malaysia. We had many foreign buyers."

"Impressive," he said absently. "Then, why were you working as a waitress?"

"That was later ,after my family were killed."

"You mentioned your father became involved with the black market," Darius added. Moriah nodded. "What were the events that led to your family's death?"

She disliked his arrogant gaze as it moved leisurely over her in appraisal. His tongue was to sharp and his approach to direct Moriah thought disdainfully. She wasn't sure she wanted to answer anymore of his questions.

He pressed her for answers. "How did you manage to escape?"

"I was visiting my friend, Kisha, in Chinatown that night. When we discovered what happened that night, Kisha told everyone I perished with my family in the fire. I thought it wise to drop out of sight."

Darius knew this must be painful for her just the same he rationalized they would discuss the matter at some point. Forging ahead he asked, "Was there someone special?" When she shot him a perplexed look, Darius explained. "A man in your country?"

"There were several suitors. No one suitable."

"Suitable?"

"There are many poor people in my country, uneducated. I wanted security and a good life."

"I see." His tone was low and clipped, now. What did he expect? At least she was honest about her motives he considered.

"And you want a woman to bear your children," she pointed out, accusation laced her voice.

"I see we understand one another," Darius said with a forced smile.

Moriah longed to wipe the smug look off his face. "I will honor the contract," she said tartly.

Their motives unveiled Darius should have felt better, regretfully he did not. "It is late, we should go." Darius rose from his chair.

The trip to *The Flying M Ranch* was made in silence.

"We should go to the market for food staples," Moriah reminded him.

"Tomorrow." His reply was succinct, his eyes now trained on the road. Moriah turned to look out the passenger window.

Becoming acquainted with Darius would not be easy she reasoned. Each time she tried to get close, he was aloof. She simply could not figure him.

~* * * *~

CHAPTER 5

Moriah was calm by the time they arrived at the ranch. She decided it was safe to ask him about his hobbies, interests and favorite foods. No doubt she would avoid future discussion of their motives for the arrangement since this was a sore subject. She hoped he would relax the ram-rod posture she recalled when the subject was mentioned. Claiming fatigue, Moriah went to bed early that night

Darius was relieved when she excused herself and went to bed, he felt on edge. Each time he thought of her innocence and eagerness to please, Darius was reminded how cynical he had become. He figured he made a mistake taking a woman fifteen years younger as a wife.

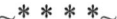

~* * * *~

Two weeks passed since he brought her to the ranch. Today they woke at six-thirty. Moriah did adhere to the schedule he implemented and this pleased Darius. Things were moving ahead as planned. He started for the coffee maker, however she beat him to it. Darius was not accustomed to having a woman underfoot. Presently Moriah urged him to take a seat at the table and she began to wait on him.

He decided to review the day's itinerary. Moriah nodded each time he mentioned tasks assigned to her. "You forgot to feed the chickens yesterday," he reminded, "and Moriah, I have asked you time and again to save the receipts for any purchases. How can we maintain a budget when you will not cooperate? Where's the ...? Oops!" He leaned down to clean the coffee spilt on the floor.

She moved to his side wondering why Darius was tense. "You are impatient with me," Moriah offered. "But I will learn." She gazed down for a moment, then cast him a bewildered look.

Darius had no idea why he had gone out of his way to be demanding. She always submitted to his wishes without complaint. The problem was she submitted too easily and this grated on him. Those big brownish-black eyes of hers reflected innocence and an eagerness to please. Darius kicked himself, he was a heel. If his life was ideal, why was he miserable?

The transition to a new lifestyle was proving more difficult than he thought. He had lived alone perhaps too long for this to work. He missed Fort Bragg and Ben. Darius's thoughts began to wander. He recalled when he and Ben broke into the nurses' quarters. And the night they stole booze from the Captain's private stock and drank to the point they could barely stand the next day. Because he was the General's son his punishment was lenient. Each time he was transferred to another station. At last he saw the error of his ways and conformed to military regulations. Whereas Ben refused to change, he was always into mischief. Maybe this was the reason he had remained a Lieutenant? Ben told Darius he had become a stuffed-shirt, nevertheless they remained friends.

When Darius was younger he strived to fulfil everyone's expectations of him; like marrying Julie, General Cunningham's daughter. Julie expressed more than a casual interest in him but

Darius held her at bay. He could not bring himself to feel otherwise. He considered Julie attractive and intelligent, just the same he found the relationship lacking. For him, the relationship went no further than friendship. As a result Darius questioned his ability for commitment.

The hurt and distrust ran deeper than he realized. The other men teased him relentlessly when he stopped dating Julie but when Darius held firm, everyone accepted his decision. To his credit Darius reminded himself he was a forty-three year old man who had commanded hundreds of men during his military career and received several medals and honorable mention. He would remain in control of the situation and he would not forget this. Women were not to be trusted, he vowed never to fall victim to their ploys.

Why couldn't he sleep? Darius thought gazing out the window. The moon was full tonight no wonder, he thought with a smile. He lifted the cup of hot chocolate to his lips. Startled by a sudden noise, Darius swung his head around as he pivoted in the chair.

Moriah stood in the doorway. Her tousled hair covered half of her patrician face. The blue satin gown she wore outlined every feminine curve. A strap skimmed invitingly over one shoulder, exposing the swell of one breast. When he turned the cup fell, spilling its contents over the floor and him.

"Damn!" Darius barked. She rushed to his side bending to retrieve the broken pieces. He leaned forward as Moriah descended and for an extended moment, they drank in the sight of one another.

She noticed he moved a hand to his mouth, sucking his forefinger. When he lowered it, she could see it the burn. A transfixed expression on his face, he no longer seemed aware of it. How was an involuntary gesture so provocative? Moriah wondered. She wanted to take his finger in her mouth while she ran hers through the dark whirl of hair on his chest.

"You're hurt," Moriah uttered softly and rose.

Darius stood at the same time. His body screamed to be as close as possible to this exotic woman. His senses ignited like brush fire. Her voluptuous breasts were soft and inviting. He could feel her nipples tickle his chest.

Why was his hand trembling? Moriah wondered as she examined it.

Now that they were inches apart, he could turn slightly and she would be on the table. He yearned to tear her gown to her waist and luxuriate in the taste and feel of her.

His eyes were that of a predator. With bravado, she brought his hand to her mouth.

"A kiss will make it better?" he taunted, his eyes daring her to take what she wanted.

Moriah knew he did not expect an answer. She moved closer, taking his finger into her mouth. Her movements were slow and deliberate.

His pulse raced in his veins, subsequently his loins throbbed. Darius lost control. He gripped her upper arms, hauling her to him. His mouth covered hers in a heartbeat. The scent of jasmine wafted sweetly in the air, further titillating his senses. For someone inexperienced, she responded like a pro -- pliant in his embrace. Darius clasped the nape of her neck with one hand, while the other moved her hips closer. His lips caressed the hollow of her neck with practiced ease as well as the swell of each breast, then he lifted his head. Gently he pushed each strap from her shoulders as she edged onto the table.

Fearful of breaking the spell, Moriah remained silent. His hooded eyes darkened as her gown slithered to her erect nipples. Darius released an appreciative moan. He stood for a moment, gazing at her perfection. After flicking the bodice of her gown with his thumb, it fell to her waist.

Unknowingly she was fulfilling his fantasy Darius thought.

Craving his touch she leaned back her arms extended behind her on the table for support. The movement sent her breasts forward.

Darius reasoned he denied himself long enough, his head dipped.

She could not move close enough, she arched her back.

He straddled her thighs in a wide stance. Cupping her bottom with both hands, he moved her forward on the table. Darius thought he was in heaven. The only thing better would be if he were sheathed inside her warm inviting body.

Moriah could not think, only follow her instincts. The sensation of flesh against flesh bombarded her sensibilities. She could feel the thrust of his manhood against her thigh.

He was consumed with desire when her soft breasts and nipples grazed the sensitive hairs on his chest. Darius swept her into his arms and carried her to the bedroom. Moriah clung to his neck, burying her face in his chest as he climbed the stairs.

Once he removed her gown, his eyes were almost reverent in their appraisal of her body. He buried his face in her bosom and laid her gently onto the bed. He had denied himself longer than most men could bear, he wanted her, now.

Moriah lifted her eyes to meet his. This was the moment she had waited for, she would be his in every sense of the word.

Darius discarded his pajamas and climbed into bed. He turned to his side, and slid across the sheet. She trembled as their bodies met. Darius brushed an errant wisp of hair from her face, then cupped her cheek in one hand and gazed deeply into her eyes. Slowly his lips moved in feathery strokes over hers. He sensed her inexperience and wanted to please her. He swept a hand lightly along her cheek to her breasts in a caressing stroke, lingering at her nipples for a moment, circling each. He shifted to the plane of her stomach then down to touch each hip and thigh. When he touched her breasts, a tiny gasping sound escaped her.

She blossomed in his palm as though her body reached out to him. His lips followed the same path tempting, urging and tantalizing her onward.

When she could bear this no longer, Moriah became bold. She wanted to awaken his body to the same fever pitch. Following his lead, she caressed, teased and tortured him with her lips and hands until he released an involuntary groan.

She was molten, sweet and ready, he poised himself over her and moved one thigh to part hers. His rigid shaft teased her moist feminine core at first with light strokes. When she thought she could endure no longer, he thrust once into her. She cried out in pain. He remained still for an extended moment. He had waited too long to possess her. Moriah was warm and tight around him. She relaxed her posture and he began to slowly rock his hips, savoring the sensation. He plunged deeper with each stroke.

Moriah never knew pleasure like this existed, she moaned his name. She threw her hips forward as he plunged downward. Enraptured she thrashed her head from side to side. He gave new meaning to the word passion.

Just as he increased the tempo building to the final blast of their sensibilities, Darius held himself stiff for a moment, and collapsed against her. She cupped his derriere in both hands, drawing him farther inside, unwilling for them to part. Moriah kissed him fervently then moved to trail kisses on each cheek. A satisfied smile spread on his face. Neither offered to move, the throbbing pulsations remained.

Later Moriah observed his breathing became slow and regular. She craned her neck to see Darius was asleep. She gave a half turn and nudged him over in bed. His eyes remained closed as he moved onto his back. Smiling she reached over and swept the damp hair from his brow. When she touched him once more, he turned his back. She drew the sheet to cover his shoulders.

If this was an example of what she had missed being single, she planned to make up for lost time. Darius was an incredible lover and worth waiting for. She hoped it had been as good for him. Moriah felt warm and tingly down to her toes as she slipped into her gown for the night.

~* * * *~

It was ten o'clock on Saturday morning when the alarm went off. Darius dropped his legs to the side of the bed and sat for a moment, willing his body to move. He blinked, trying to clear his bleary vision. Today he planned to collect the puppies in Austin and pick up the supplies they needed for the ranch. After breakfast Darius and Moriah drove leisurely to Austin. Their first stop was the market, second the feed store, and their last stop before leaving town was the pet shop.

The pet store owner supplied a pet carrier for the puppies. Moriah giggled when one of them licked her squarely on the nose. "They're adorable!" she exclaimed when first she laid eyes on them.

Smiling, Darius watched her play with the pups, stealing a glimpse now and again as he drove home. He wanted to know more about Moriah. Their mutual interest in starting a new life together concerned Darius. He knew each wanted to feel needed and loved. He would strive to know her better.

Last night Darius had never enjoyed a woman more. Indeed he was fortunate in finding her. Moriah was truly something special. All the more reason he planned to hold a tight rein on the situation. He would not let on she had penetrated his resolve. This would be a fatal mistake.

Part of him wanted to trust Moriah and allow himself to be vulnerable. Given the situation he feared loss of control. No one had ever needed him before, until he met Moriah. She was innocent in appearance and passionate. She was beautiful, soft spoken, and her sinewy limbs no doubt Darius lusted for Moriah. He was determined if this worked out, he wanted her love as well. He envisioned her weak with longing for him, as he was for her. Each time he thought of Moriah, Darius became hard. This could prove embarrassing he thought.

He hadn't known anyone to be so vital and sweeping in their influence of others. Moriah was truly like the wind. She filled his thoughts most days and this made him uncomfortable. He disliked being vulnerable. A man could endure just so much. When one at last acquired something they desired, why was it frightening? Darius gave a shaky, low laugh.

Another part of him distrusted and feared Moriah. Darius could not afford another heartbreak. He suspected he might easily lose his heart to her. He refused to allow this. He remembered what happened the last time he trusted a woman. The pain helped to harden his heart. Next time Moriah would be the one to seek him out.

In spite of everything he had a good time today Darius thought checking the horses in the barn. He was amazed the way they exchanged looks only lovers could. This was out of character for him he considered. Later that afternoon Moriah was stirring a pot on the stove. Darius could not identify the wonderful aroma. Unaware of his presence, she did not turn around.

He came up behind her. "Find the picnic basket," he suggested.

Moriah lifted her brows in question. "Are we going somewhere?"

"You might say that." With this, he turned and walked out the back door.

Now would be an excellent time for them to become acquainted. Most of the time he wanted to crush her to him. Her soft feminine curves and her heart-shaped mouth drove him to the brink -- it begged to be kissed. Darius yearned to run his fingers through the tumble of waves at her nape. He yearned to see her eyes drugged from his lovemaking.

Nevertheless the old wounds resurfaced. Nancy's betrayal reminded him to maintain his distance. Women were not to be trusted. She had made him a laughingstock. He would never forget their last meeting. The pain he suspected would never go away. Darius saddled the horses and led them from the barn. He enjoyed the outdoors and this was an extraordinary day.

Moriah closed the basket when he strode inside. The screen door banged behind him as it contacted the door jamb

"You'll need boots," he instructed hurriedly.

She glanced at her feet. "Why?"

"Your sandals will not last five minutes on a horse."

Moriah managed to swallow after a moment in spite of the clenched muscles in her stomach. "But I cannot ride." Her brows wrinkled together. Staring up at him, she set the basket on the butcher's block with a thud.

"Cannot or will not?" Darius challenged, surprised by her response. He waited for further explanation.

"Cannot," Moriah repeated. "I have not had the opportunity to learn."

~* * * *~

 **CHAPTER 6**

Pleased he misjudged her, he released the sigh he had unconsciously held. The corners of his mouth slowly curled into a smile. "We'll ride double," he instructed. "Now, get your boots." Moriah nodded and left the room. He paused for a moment before retrieving his guitar from the closet.

Darius mounted the Appaloosa in one swift movement, then reined the horse over to the porch where Moriah stood. Leaning to his side, he swung her into place behind him. She clung tightly to his waist. His guitar hung from the saddle horn on the other side. "Hold tight." His heels briskly contacted the horse's flanks. The Appaloosa began a slow cantor.

Moriah felt as though she was in an old western on television. This was cozy, she thought. Moriah could feel the heated strength of him. He moved as one with the graceful animal. Cumulus clouds dotted the sky with various shades of blue against the afternoon sky. The landscape seemed to rush by.

Regardless of the cantor, Moriah held steadfast to him and the picnic basket. She hoped the contents would not spill over. A considerable distance from the farmhouse, Darius pulled back on the reins, encouraging the animal to stop.

"How picturesque. I do not recall the lake," Moriah said appreciatively.

"I waited to show you until we cleared the area," Darius explained. Several tall trees surrounded the lake, creating a tranquil atmosphere.

Perhaps he has a romantic nature after all? Moriah would give anything if he would abandon the reserved mask and confide in her just once. Most of all she wanted him to take her in those strong, capable arms of his and make slow, passionate love right on the grass - until both were weak and senseless. Darius was the most attractive man she had ever seen, when he smiled his whole face and demeanor softened. Watching him made her knees weak.

"This is the reason you were late coming home the last two weeks?" she queried.

Darius nodded as a grin spread on his face. "I wanted to surprise you."

He dismounted the Appaloosa after lowering Moriah to her feet. The way she slid off the horse and down his body made his heart palpitate. Instantly Darius set her from him, refusing to make a fool of himself. She was a real lady. He wanted her approval, somehow he needed it.

Darius led the horse to water and tethered it to a nearby tree. He chose a beautiful area under a towering oak tree for the picnic. Moriah spread the blanket on a grassy area and set the basket down. She began to unpack its contents.

How would she respond if he took her right here? Would she submit or slap his face? Darius was surprised by his growing interest in Moriah. Barring this, he was anxious to start a family.

After all, he wanted a son. Darius sauntered toward her his guitar in hand.

His serene expression pleased Moriah.

He uncorked the bottle of red wine and poured each a glass. She unwrapped what appeared as a cluster of rice on a leaf. Shifting his gaze to her, he grimaced. "What is this?"

"Oh! It is nasi lemak." She smiled reassuringly. "This is good."

If she expected him to eat this, she had better think again! "I'm sure it's tasty." He obliged her with a smile.

"Here try it." Moriah shoved it into his hands.

Darius stared down at it for a moment as if he considered it poison. He lifted his head. "What's in it?"

"Coconut rice with spicy condiment, egg, cucumber and fish." Moriah took a hearty bite of hers.

Whatever it was, gross was a mild word for it he thought. Steeling himself against probable indigestion, he tentatively tasted it. Pleasantly intrigued with the new food, he took a sip of wine.

"Try kctupat, it's a Malay rice cake."

He watched Moriah eat, her movements were graceful to say the least. He was fond of her expressive eyes and those heart-shaped lips. At that moment her tongue swept out to capture an errant strand of rice on her cheek. This simple movement inspired him to press his lips to hers. He suppressed his libido. He glanced down smiling to himself before he said, "What was it like growing up in Malaysia?"

"My childhood was care free. My people are reserved and formally polite. We believe in strong family ties. I grew up within the close confines of my family - my uncles, aunts, and cousins."

"Sounds wonderful." He laid back on the blanket, folding his arms behind his head. He could get used to the sight of her.

"It was." Moriah sipped her wine.

"What is your favorite sport?"

"Basketball."

"Mine is football. I will not ask your favorite food. I probably wouldn't know what it was," Darius chuckled. Her face was radiant when she smiled. He swallowed hard and continued. "How do men and women meet in your country?"

"Most young people do not go out alone. They meet in groups in public places. Couples who walk hand-in-hand in public are frowned upon."

She appeared sad. "What's wrong?" Darius lifted her chin with his thumb.

"I regret, I am unable to bring a dowry." Her eyes were sad. "That is what you call it?"

"I'm not concerned with a dowry," he answered softly. He reached for the guitar and began to strum a lively tune. Darius was amazed by the new emotions he experienced. He wanted to protect her and to somehow lift her spirits.

Moriah realized they were worlds apart in upbringing. She learned Darius's father was rarely home as he grew up. He learned to be self-reliant, whereas Moriah enjoyed the love and support of her family. She had no problem expressing her emotions, whereas this was foreign to him. The differing attitudes toward marriage and family were evident between them. Darius explained his father and the tragic marriage taught him otherwise -- nothing was forever. They could learn a great deal from one another Moriah considered.

She remembered her mother taught her, "The man is head of the family. But his wife is supreme law inside the home."

Moriah wondered if she possessed the fortitude to stand up to Darius? She decided she would deal with this issue later. Indeed Moriah's parents loved their children. Her chest tightened with emotion as she swallowed back the lump in her throat. Tears welled in her eyes with the thought she would never see them again.

Why had her eyes suddenly filled with tears? Darius wondered. Perhaps the melancholy music affected her in the same way? He decided now was a good time to change the subject. "Would you care to do some target practice?"

"I would not. Where I grew up, we had no need of guns," Moriah explained.

"Then its time you learned." He rose and ambled toward the Appaloosa. He removed something from the saddle bag and returned to her side. "It's a 38 special. A good gun for you to learn with."

"I do not like guns."

"With the closest neighbor miles away, you should learn to defend yourself," he insisted.

He walked off in the distance and placed several rocks in a pile. "Aim over there." He passed her the gun after checking it was properly loaded.

"But --" she cajoled.

"You're right. We shouldn't practice when we have been drinking." He put it away.

Moriah released a deep sigh. "Play something on the guitar?" she encouraged, nudging him toward the picnic area.

Darius sat Indian style on the blanket and strummed the guitar. He played a series of songs for her. He couldn't be sure if the tranquil mood was because of his wife or the music. He simply decided to enjoy the moment.

When he accidentally hit a sour note, he laughed and she joined in. His laughter was contagious she thought he should smile more. Moriah asked him about his army career. A deep affection filled his voice as Darius described his relationship with a close army buddy, Benjamin Willis. He explained that Ben was an orphan for lack of family or direction, he entered the Point -- later, the army. They became friends immediately and from that time they remained close. Moriah knew he missed Ben. Darius looked as though he were a million miles away as he related this.

Where had the afternoon gone she wondered glancing at her watch. She recalled the delightful animation that covered his face when he described their shenanigans in the service. Why had he remained unattached for years? It would soon be dark at eight o'clock, they began to gather the picnic supplies and headed for the ranch. Moriah ruminated what he shared with her earlier as they rode back to the ranch. There was a quiet determination about him, however her curiosity failed to be satisfied. She sensed Darius resented his father's absence during the years he grew up. He spoke lovingly of his mother and sister. Moriah could not bring herself to ask about Nancy, the woman he married earlier.

She couldn't bear the thought of another woman in his arms. When he chose to speak of Nancy his voice became defiant. The ride back to the ranch was in silence. The afternoon was pleasant although it raised several questions in Moriah's mind. Time was the key. Her husband closely guarded his privacy, but she managed to persuade him to share a part of himself. She would respect this and wait for him to offer more.

When they returned to the ranch Darius eased her off the horse onto the porch, then he led the Appaloosa into the barn. He was convinced he would guard his emotions closely where Moriah was concerned. She could hurt him deeply if he allowed her to get close.

Minutes later Moriah heard Darius enter the house as she hurriedly slipped into her negligee. Moriah was indecisive whether to join him or simply go to bed, instead she paced back and forth in the bedroom. Several minutes later, she grabbed a book and began to read. If he wanted her, he would have to approach first.

Darius knew their relationship had changed. What possessed him to reveal his past today? he wondered. He enjoyed her company today and felt he could trust her to a point. Suddenly he found himself looking for reasons not to sleep with her. He refused to admit he needed anyone. In the past his vulnerability cost him dearly. Darius suspected if he gave Moriah half a chance she could break his heart, irreparably this time he feared. He was not prepared to take the risk, not yet.

Weary of reading after an hour, Moriah switched off the bedside lamp. Darius never approached and this both confused and frustrated her. She couldn't believe her husband hadn't offered to make love. She possessed the same desires and needs of most women. Americans have ironic ideas related to marriage she considered. Moriah was reared to respect a man. Her idea of a husband was someone to love, protect and share her hopes and expectations of a loving family and home. She was accustomed to strong-willed men. When Darius failed to share her bed tonight, Moriah found this humiliating.

~* * * *~

Moriah rose reluctantly as the sun beckoned a warm July morning. Her sleep last night was restless. Clad in her robe she padded into the kitchen. The aroma of coffee was obvious as she entered the kitchen. She noted the pile of dirty dishes in the sink. Turning, she discovered a note propped on the butcher's block that read:

Moriah, Jason and I left earlier than usual today. We have considerable work to complete. Enjoy your day. See you for lunch. Darius

She crumpled the note in one hand and threw it in the trash. He signed the note simply Darius and this incensed her. She told herself she might as well be hired help for all he cared. Moriah went back to bed wondering what it would take to penetrate his barrier.

The telephone rang, startling Moriah.

"Hello. I am Carrie Hanks." When no response followed, she continued, "Darius's sister."

"Forgive me," she responded. "My name is Moriah."

"I know." Carrie paused. "How's Darius holding up?"

Moriah wondered what was meant by the remark? "He is fine. I am afraid he is out on the ranch somewhere."

"That's okay. I wanted to speak with you," Carrie explained. "I'm sorry I was unable to attend your wedding. My son, Chris was ill."

"I understand." Moriah waited.

"He caught the flu just before we planned to leave," Carrie continued. "I realize this is short notice but my parents and I would like to visit. It would give everyone the opportunity to get acquainted. What do you think?" Moriah remained silent. "Moriah?"

"I agree," she managed reluctantly.

"Oh, and one more thing, please don't mention this to Darius?"

"This will be our secret."

"I hope this isn't inconvenient?" Carrie queried.

"Not at all," Moriah replied, anxiously. "Everyone is welcome. When will you arrive?"

"Let's see, today is Sunday, in one week. This should allow ample time to prepare."

"You will honor our home."

"Thank you. I look forward to meeting you. I couldn't think of a better time since this will be Darius's birthday." Carrie rang off.

Peculiar Moriah thought, he never mentioned his birthday coming up.

True to her word, Moriah never uttered a word to Darius about his family's plan to visit on his birthday. She hoped his family would like her. Seemingly Darius regarded her as a possession, not as his wife and this displeased Moriah. Perhaps with his family's influence she might feel she belonged.

~****~

The sun shined brightly overhead she noticed looking out the kitchen window. Moriah prepared a variety of Malay foods today for Darius's birthday. She had trouble believing he would be forty-four. Completing the tasks at hand, she washed her hands and removed her apron. Everything was perfect!

She reflected her riding lessons began four days ago. The shooting lessons would soon begin. Even though she was not particularly fond of riding and shooting, the lessons allowed her time with her husband. Lamar's wife, Nora visited yesterday. Apparently Nora was abreast of the local happenings. The two women visited for two hours. Nora mentioned the local women's groups, quilting and ceramics classes available. In addition, Moriah learned square dance classes were offered. Then Nora announced she had to leave, assuring Moriah they would visit again soon.

Snatching herself to the present, Moriah looked forward to when Darius would return home. He gave her life purpose and she missed him. It was hot today she considered surely he would be home soon. Moriah dropped into a rocking chair on the porch and set it in motion. This morning Darius mentioned in his note that he and Jason would mend fences. This would require most of the day but the repairs were almost complete. He never once let on, today was his birthday.

~****~

CHAPTER 7

The July sun blazed overhead and Moriah pulled her moist hair atop her head with a ribbon. The Mc Coy family was scheduled to arrive today. The four bedroom house was more than ready for their guests. Moriah was both anxious and fretful about meeting his family. True she briefly met his parents at the wedding but this was different she would have to entertain them. Why were they were late in their arrival? And where was Darius? He and Jason should have returned long ago.

Finally Darius and Jason drove up in the yard. When they climbed out of the truck Moriah noticed how dirty and weary they appeared, she waved. Jason started for the bunkhouse, as Darius approached the farmhouse.

"How was your day?" Darius smiled, climbing the porch.

"It was productive. Dinner is ready," Moriah replied. "Did you complete what you planned to do today?"

"Yes, we did. I'm starved," he began. "I'll shower and be out in a few minutes and we'll have dinner." He leaned to kiss her cheek, before entering the house. She followed him inside.

Moriah opted to bath and put on a nice dress for dinner. The Mc Coys could arrive anytime she told herself.

A sound outside brought Darius to the window to investigate as a green Taurus station wagon pulled into the driveway. The Mc Coys were here.

"It's my parents, Carrie and her son Chris." Darius smiled incredulously. He stepped into his deck shoes and hurried out the door. Moriah walked to the doorway and waited.

"I can't believe you're here." Darius slapped Seth McCoy's back.

"We thought it was time for a proper visit," Seth answered.

"Sweetheart, you look well." Rebecca McCoy embraced her son and pulled back s lightly. "Let me have a look at you. You've put on a few pounds."

Darius's eyes moved to his waistline. He shot his mother a sideward look and laughed, moving an arm around her shoulders as they approached the porch.

Seth gathered a sleeping child in arms and followed close behind them. Carrie smiled and reached behind the driver's seat and withdrew an overnight bag. She fell into step alongside her father.

Moriah moved aside to allow them entry. "Welcome to our home."

"Thank you, Moriah," Rebecca McCoy greeted. Her daughter-in-law followed them inside, and everyone exchanged embraces. Darius directed the women into the living room. He excused himself to show Seth the guest rooms.

The men joined the women in the living room after putting Chris to bed.

"What a pleasant surprise," Darius repeated in amazement. Straddling a dining chair, he turned the chair's back to his guests, his fingers intertwined, his chin resting on his hands.

"We couldn't forget your birthday," Carrie said pleasantly. "It's as good a reason as any to visit."

"I'm flattered."

"You're forty-four today, right?" Carrie added.

"Thanks for reminding me." Darius chuckled. He was pleased to see his family.

"Moriah, it's about time someone settled him down," Rebecca interjected. He daughter-in-law smiled timidly. "Seth is Chris still asleep?"

"He's still sawing Z's."

"Darius help your father carry the bags in," Rebecca said with practiced ease. "He's not what he used to be."

"I resent that!" Seth said mockingly. Darius rose.

"Is Chris your only child?" Moriah asked.

"Yes. He makes me think of Darius," Carrie supplied.

"What is his age?" Moriah continued.

"Five."

Everyone appeared tense Moriah considered. It was always stressful to meet new people this she understood. She smiled but inside it hurt because Darius had not confided today was his birthday. When had he planned to tell her? "Anyone care for lemonade?"

Everyone agreed the drink would be welcome. Carrie volunteered to help.

Once they were in the kitchen Carrie raved, "You can keep a secret. My brother was blown away."

"I respected your wishes." Moriah paused. "Why did he choose not to tell me it was his birthday?"

"Maybe he didn't want you to think you married an old man?" Carrie chuckled.

"He is more than attractive. Old?" Moriah shrugged her shoulders in disbelief. "Never."

"I agree but Darius is self-conscious about his age."

"You mean he's vain?"

"You could say that."

"Did your husband accompany you?"

"Frank was killed in an auto accident two years ago."

"I did not mean to pry."

Carrie was quiet for a moment as if reflecting, then she spoke in a steady voice. "We'd better serve the lemonade before they come to search for us."

She was unlike Darius in every way. Whereas Darius's demeanor was serious, Carrie was mischievous. Her sandy hair, fair complexion and blue eyes were in direct contrast with Darius's dark features. The two of them might have had different parents Moriah considered.

Seth and Darius by this time had emptied the car of luggage when Carrie entered the living room with Darius's birthday cake alight with candles.

"For chrissakes." Darius heaved a deep sigh, shaking his head. Momentarily everyone turned to the sound of approaching footsteps as Ben Willis entered the room.

"I forgot to mention Darius," Moriah began, "Ben arrived just before your family arrived. Since you were dressing for dinner, I showed him to his room to unpack and settle in." Darius's face brightened with the sight of his dear friend.

Carrie sighed, placing the cake on the coffee table, her eyes trained on Ben. Standing she lifted both arms as a conductor before an orchestra. "Okay, everyone --"

"Hold on," Darius interrupted, "Everyone knows Ben, except Carrie." He gestured with his hands, "I'd like you to meet my best friend, Lieutenant Benjamin Willis, Carrie." Darius loved to watch Carrie squirm he knew she was taken aback. Ben wasn't bad looking and she could do worse Darius considered. "Ben, this is my sister, Carrie."

Ben smiled in acknowledgement of Carrie and moved to Darius's side as everyone sang 'Happy Birthday.' Darius blew out the candles with one attempt. With an exaggerated puff, he exhaled audibly.

Rebecca moved to her son's side, embracing him she kissed his cheek. "This was your idea!" Darius accused mockingly.

"Guilty," Rebecca pleaded. Darius returned her kiss with one of his own. "Were you genuinely surprised, son?"

"Yes, mother. Thank you," Darius replied. While everyone visited over cake and coffee he opened the presents.

"What an unexpected pleasure," Moriah began, her eyes engaging Darius's. "It seems you neglected to mention your birthday." He gave a helpless shrug.

Ben watched the interactions around him, however he couldn't take his eyes off Carrie. So this was Darius's sister? Wow! He had a sudden urge to take up residence in Arizona. He couldn't help but notice she observed him with the same intent expression. Ben suspected this trip would prove to be more than interesting. He moved in Carrie's direction.

"So you're Darius's sister?" Ben drawled.

"I've been accused of worse things," Carrie managed. She felt her face color. "I've heard Darius mention you. How nice to meet you at last."

"Darius has been holding out on me. How did he manage to keep you under wraps?"

"I've lived away from the family for some time," Carrie explained.

Ben decided he would become acquainted with Carrie while everyone watched Darius open the gifts.

"Are you married?" Ben ventured.

He certainly did not waste time, Carrie thought. "No."

Ben's heart soared.

"When Frank was killed two years ago, Chris and I moved to Arizona."

Rats! Ben thought, she has a boyfriend. "Who is Chris?"

"My son."

Ben released the breath he hadn't realized he held. He could feel everyone's eyes on them.

"It seems Carrie and Ben have become fast friends," Darius teased. "Hey, we're opening presents here."

"Okay, okay." Ben blushed. Carrie stood and moved to join the others.

Carrie and Moriah were engaged in conversation, when Rebecca approached.

"Moriah, you have the house looking spectacular. A woman's touch goes a long way in making a house a home."

"Thank you, Mrs. McCoy."

"Nonsense. Call me Rebecca." The two women embraced.

"How are you finding life here compared to Malaysia?" Carrie ventured to change the subject.

"Easier. I clean after one man instead of many.

Rebecca almost chocked on her drink. "Many?"

"It's not as if she believes in polygamy, mother. I'm sure you misunderstood." Both women shifted their gaze to Moriah.

"What I mean to say is, I worked as a waitress in an Inn." Moriah's gaze moved from Carrie to Rebecca, waiting for a response.

"I'm sorry," Rebecca offered. "I meant no offense."

"None taken."

"How's married life?" Carrie prodded. She noticed Ben had moved to where the men were gathered in animated conversation. Carrie smiled to herself.

Carrie listened half-heartedly. Moriah's eyes followed Carrie's gaze. She knew Carrie was focused more on what the men were saying.

"I think we are adjusting well," Moriah evaded.

"Considering you didn't know one another," Rebecca added flatly.

"Mother!" Carrie pinched Rebecca's elbow.

"It is true," Moriah conceded.

"Mommy, mommy! Where are you? " A small voice called from the other room.

"If you'll excuse me? Chris is awake," Carrie said, glaring at her mother.

"I'll attend to him," Rebecca volunteered, standing. Carrie lowered herself in the chair as Rebecca left the room.

"Mother didn't mean anything by that last remark. She tends to speak her mind."

"Please, I am not offended." Moriah pushed a trembling hand through her hair. "Tell me how long did the trip take?"

"Two days."

"No wonder the child slept so long. I hope you will honor our home by staying awhile."

"Are you sure about that?" Carrie replied.

"Excuse me?"

"Just a bad joke." Carrie lifted her brows expectantly. "Dad plans for us to stay a week."

"We are pleased to have you," Moriah answered. "It is a coincidence Ben plans to say a week as well."

Carrie was relieved Rebecca chose that moment to return with her grandson. At least she wouldn't be cornered into expressing an opinion. Ben made Carrie uncomfortable the way he kept staring at her from the corner of his eye, pretending absorption when his mind was elsewhere.

"Look who's here," Darius remarked smiling, his arms outstretched to Chris.

"Uncle Darius." Chris withdrew his hand from Rebecca's and approached. "It's your birthday, mommy said so." He noticed the cake. "Can I have a piece?"

"Of course, champ. Rebecca cut Chris some cake," Seth suggested.

Everyone gathered for Moriah's Malay dinner. Despite the unusual food everyone was enthusiastic and offered pleasant conversation throughout the meal. After dinner Rebecca and Chris joined the men in the living room while Carrie and Moriah cleared the table.

"The food was intriguing to the taste buds," Rebecca began. "I don't think I have tasted anything like it."

"It was good." Seth patted his mid-drift bulge. "I'd weigh twice as much if I ate like this all the time."

"Moriah will be pleased to hear that," Darius commented. "It took me awhile to get used to it."

"You are teaching her to cook beef stroganoff and your favorite dishes, I hope?" Rebecca questioned.

Darius considered her statement a moment." Moriah is a good cook regardless of the cuisine," he replied. Darius shifted his attention back to Chris playing with his toys on the floor. "In answer to your question, yes."

"Rebecca, keep Chris company. I want to speak with Darius," Seth instructed.

"About what?" his wife asked.

"The ranch among other things," Seth hedged.

"Ben why don't you and Carrie get acquainted?" Darius encouraged.

Ben knew this was his cue to leave and he didn't mind in the least. What an idea Ben mused inviting Carrie to join him for a walk.

"We'll be in the study, mother," Darius announced over his shoulder leaving the room.

Rebecca dismissed them with a wave of the hand, joining her grandson on the floor. Seth followed his son into the study.

"Care for a smoke?" Darius offered.

"I had to give them up. The doctor said my emphysema's getting worse."

"How about a drink?"

"Scotch on the rocks."

Darius turned to pour the drinks. "How's the arthritis?"

"I hurt in places, I never knew I had."

Darius laughed.

"Your turn is coming."

"Still grumbling as ever." Darius passed Seth his drink. "Cheers."

Lifting his glass in salute, Seth lowered himself in a padded chair. "Here's mud in your eye."

"How was the trip?"

"Considering we stopped frequently, I think we made good time," Seth commented. He sipped his scotch. "How are you settling into married life?"

Darius sat mutely, a thoughtful expression on his face.

"Regrets?"

"Not exactly."

"What then? And don't tell me everything is rosy. Save the flowery stuff for your mother."

"What makes you think something's wrong?"

"When you've been around people as long as I have been, you won't have to ask. What gives?"

Darius sipped his scotch.

Seth continued," Moriah seems to be a good wife."

"She is."

"Well?" Seth downed his drink.

"It takes time to know one another."

"Man, don't tell me you haven't bedded your wife?"

"I never said that."

"Thank heaven." Seth cleared his throat. "Clearly there's a problem. What is it?"

"You can take that look off your face right now," Darius responded, then paused for a moment. "She's so damn agreeable." He regretted the slip of the tongue immediately.

"You are not into kinky stuff?"

"Nothing like that. What I mean is she's excessively eager to serve and obey." He made a self-deprecating sound.

"No spirit, huh?"

Darius shook his head. "I had no idea how it would effect me."

"Sometimes I wish your mother was more agreeable. She gives me 'what for' regularly but we have fun making up."

"When you married mother has she always done exactly what you've asked?"

"Hell, no. I wasn't interested in marriage at first but Becky managed to convince me otherwise." Seth gave a sentimental snort. "Bored?"

"I wouldn't say that." Darius shot Seth a frustrated look.

"Romance her. Give it some time, you'll figure it out." Seth draped an arm around his son's shoulders. "We'd better join the others."

When Seth and Darius rejoined the others the women were visiting in the living room. Chris was building a skyscraper on the floor.

"He's a good boy," Moriah remarked.

"You should see him at home," Rebecca teased. "A totally different kid." Chris ignored her comment.

Moriah smiled and sat mutely.

"Do you plan to have children?" queried Rebecca.

"A man needs a son," Darius supplied entering the room with Seth. Moriah's frown changed to a smile. From the look on his mother's face, she was clearly bemused.

Rebecca sensed trouble. A diversion was requisite she thought. Consequently Rebecca explained during her husband's stint in the service, the Mc Coys lived abroad for many years. For good measure she proceeded to entertain everyone with amusing stories of Darius's childhood.

~* * * *~

CHAPTER 8

Moriah was taken aback when she almost collided with Carrie in the kitchen the next morning. The aroma of fresh coffee wafted in the air.

"Join me in a cup," Carrie said more a statement than a request.

"Darius expects breakfast to be ready," Moriah murmured."I'll have mine while --"

"Let him wait." Carrie gestured to a stool. "Sit!"

"He'll be angry."

"It won't be the first time."

"But --"

"Save it. Have some coffee."

Moriah yielded to Carrie's will. "You are not a trained seal. You're his wife."

Moriah was uneasy just the same she would enjoy lingering over coffee.

"I see my brother has been playing Colonel, again."

Carrie's attitude perplexed her. "He is a Colonel."

"In the army, not in his home. How's he treating you anyway?"

"Fine."

"And you cater to him."

"He's my husband."

"You poor thing," Carrie said clucking her tongue as shook her head in disapproval.

With a scowl, Darius entered the room. Undoubtedly, he heard every word. "This is not your concern, Carrie."

Moriah was dumbfounded.

"Breakfast is cereal, fresh fruit and toast," Carrie said blithely. "Help yourself." She threw Darius a loaf of bread.

"I am warning you, Carrie!" His swarthy face turned scarlet.

Carrie cast him an exaggerated grin. "That's my name."

Moriah's eyes vacillated between Darius and Carrie for several moments.

Darius crossed over to the toaster and dropped two slices of bread inside. He opened the cupboard and filled a bowl with raisin bran. Moriah started to help him but Carrie firmly clutched her elbow. Moments later Darius removed fresh fruit and milk from the refrigerator and took a seat at the table.

Carrie stood and approached the coffeemaker. "Coffee anyone?"

Darius shot her a derisive look.

Moriah requested a refill. Carrie leisurely refilled the cups and spoke casually to her brother. "I see you haven't had your first cup. Let me do the honors."

Glaring at Carrie, Darius remained silent. Carrie filled a cup and set it before her brother. Leisurely she returned to her seat.

He made short work of breakfast. Grumbling under his breath, Darius left slamming the screen door behind him.

"You see, he's angry."

"He's not the only one," Carrie said tartly.

Bewildered by the exchange, Moriah began to clear the table.

"Moriah, you have a lot to learn about men," Carrie said leaving the room.

Carrie's last statement bothered Moriah. She didn't know what to make of their behavior. Their body language belied their congeniality. It was confusing. Maybe she should have remained in Malaysia?

Seth and Rebecca stepped into the kitchen as Carrie left in a huff.

"What's with her?" Rebecca asked with a glance over her shoulder.

"If I didn't know better, I'd say Carrie's been at it with Darius," Seth remarked.

"Are all Americans so volatile?" Moriah blurted with a deep sigh.

"No. But our children are," Seth admitted. "They take after their mother," he commented with a chuckle. Rebecca gave him a look of disapproval.

"What were they fighting about?" Rebecca queried hesitantly.

"I'm not sure," Moriah answered.

"Any coffee left, Becky?" Seth said, trying to change the subject.

"Plenty," Moriah said blankly.

"Those two have fought since they were kids," Seth supplied. "Don't let them upset you, Moriah. Thirty minutes from now they won't remember what it was about."

"Do you really think so?"

"I speak from experience." Seth wrapped an arm around his daughter-in-law. She looked as though she might burst into tears at any moment. Seth considered she has a new husband, a new country and a new culture. This was a great deal for anyone to digest at once. Damn, Darius. They had spoiled him terribly. His son's behavior toward his wife disappointed Seth. He reasoned Darius was ungrateful. With Moriah in tow, Seth insisted she take a seat next to him. He poured coffee for each of them and settled himself on a stool.

Perceptively, Rebecca wanted to cheer her daughter-in-law. She complimented Moriah on her management of all the house guests.

"I do not understand Darius," Moriah admitted reluctantly. Tears welled in her eyes.

"Our son is a good man. He's just confused," Rebecca said softly. "I think he's trying to adjust to the new situation. Being single so long has not helped."

"In addition, he's been in command of hundreds of men," Seth defended. "He will come around. Give him time. This is all new to him."

Moriah wondered if they realized how she felt. "He's fortunate to have parents who love him so much." Moriah clutched Seth's and Rebecca's hands tightly in hers.

Chris skipped into the kitchen. "I'm hungry, Grandma."

Rebecca transferred her gaze to him. "What would you like?"

"Blueberry muffins."

"Sorry, baby. How about eggs, cereal and toast?"

Chris thought for a moment before answering. "Well, okay. Where's mommy?"

"Right here," Carrie said, entering the room. Moriah stood. Carrie nodded as took a seat next to Chris at the butcher block. "Where are you going, Moriah?"

"It's time I dressed." Emotionally she felt better though doubts continued to haunt her. Moriah left the room.

Shifting her gaze to Chris, Carrie said, "Hey, tiger let's go into the dining room, huh?" Chris bobbed his head.

"C 'mon, grandma and grandpa, " Chris encouraged.

Seth turned to his wife, "You girls go ahead. I'll see if I can help Darius." He crossed the room to where his wife stood at the stove and kissed her cheek. "See you for lunch." He went out the back door.

While Chris chattered over breakfast, Carrie and Rebecca tried to amuse him. "When I grow up I want to be just like Uncle Darius and have a ranch," Chris boasted.

"That's fine, dear. As long as you don't treat women the way he does," Carrie said under her breath. Rebecca glowered at her. "It's true," she supplied defensively.

"What?" Rebecca feigned ignorance, hoping to change the subject.

"He should learn women have more than two functions."

"What a horrible thing to say about your brother!"

"Someone should teach him a lesson." Carrie cupped her chin in one hand, her elbow resting on the table.

"Now ... Carrie."

"I never said I'd be the one to do it." Carrie knew her mother didn't care to hear negative comments about her son. Darius acts like some monolithic male. His five years her senior, Carrie considered he might have matured. Women have two functions as far as Darius was concerned: obeying her husband and bearing children.

Carrie had to credit brother for his ingenuity. He managed his domestic life similar to the military. It was a dirty trick but so what! Maybe a week would be sufficient time if she worked fast?

Rebecca could see the wheels turning in her daughter's head. What was Carrie up to?

~* * * *~

Two dilemmas troubled Carrie. First of all her brother was a pain in the backside. She worried his marriage wouldn't last if Darius didn't change. Second the unforeseen event of meeting Benjamin Willis was a timing issue. Ordinarily Carrie would never be attracted to a man with red hair, however his green eyes gleamed mischief and this intrigued her. No doubt she was attracted to Ben.

She recalled their walk together last night. From the moment her gaze settled on Ben, Carrie suspected the attraction was mutual. The way his eyes followed her unnerved her in delightful way. It was as though just the two of them were in the room. Ben Willis entered the scene rocking her concentration to its foundation. Carrie couldn't recall ever being attracted to a man in this way; not even Frank.

When Frank died two years ago, Carrie was determined to devote herself to raising her son. Until now, she held true to her resolve. When she was alone with Ben, they were not at a loss for words. Carrie considered it seemed they found in one another what they had searched for their whole lives.

"Darius mentioned you live in Arizona," Ben said casually as they walked in the warm Texas night air.

It was refreshing to be alone with Ben, Carrie considered.

"Yes. The house in California held too many memories after Frank died. I sold it and we moved to Tucson. I wanted a new environment to raise my son. One that was safe and where I have influence over his values."

"Impressive," Ben commented. "Carrie you're an interesting person. What is your work?"

"I'm an astronomer." Carried considered Ben more compelling than herself.

"You study the stars?"

"Exactly. I have this great telescope at home."

"Do you work at home?"

"No. I work for a major research corporation in Tucson. I love to observe and study the stars," Carrie confessed. Why was she telling him this? she wondered. "I find it relaxes me."

"Tell me about yourself," Ben encouraged.

"What would you like to know?" Carrie was at ease with Ben. Still this was unfamiliar turf for her. For once she was at loss for words!

"Is there someone special in your life?" Ben hazarded. He wanted to be the man in Carrie's life.

Carrie turned to him in amazement. Slowly a grin spread across her face. "Ben, that's personal."

"Sorry." Ben laughed. Carrie cut her eyes sideways at him.

"You don't sound as though you mean it," Carrie persisted.

"Actually, I am not."

"Do you often say things you don't mean?"

"Are you always so direct?" Ben challenged.

Carrie laughed wholeheartedly. "I refuse to answer that."

Ben liked the way Carrie made him feel. She was vivacious, direct, independent, witty and attractive. A combination he considered dangerous. He appreciated Carrie for the woman she was.

What a lucky stroke discovering Ben Carrie thought. She found herself wondering if he would be a good father. And, if Chris would like him. A new man in her life was the farthest thing from Carrie's mind, she laughed. Funny how life sneaks up and takes one by surprise she mused.

"We better go inside," Ben suggested. Carrie nodded in agreement. As they approached the porch, Ben said, "Oh, and Carrie?"

"Yes?"

"I 'd like to know you better. I think we have a lot in common." There he said it!

"Oh? In what way?" Carrie teased.

"For starters, a zest for life."

Suddenly her expression became serious. "Ben, I have a son."

"Are you saying no?"

"My son comes first in my life. Chris's happiness is important to me. I'm all he has."

"I like kids, Carrie," Ben replied, warming to the conversation. Carrie shrugged."I must have misunderstood," he said. "I thought we enjoyed one another's company."

"You're not mistaken," Carrie supplied. "I like you too, Benjamin Willis," she said before continuing inside.

Great! Ben thought. A green light.

~* * *~

CHAPTER 9

"Hold up," Ben called out the door as Darius walked purposefully past him.

Glancing over his shoulder, Darius pivoted waiting for further explanation. He was amazed to see Ben up at six in the morning. Ben had chased after Carrie like a puppy, Darius thought.

"I would like to go with you today," Ben supplied.

"Sure if you can pull yourself away?" Darius said sardonically.

"And what exactly is that supposed to mean?" If Darius wanted to play it this way, Ben would oblige him.

Darius stopped in his tracks, his back to Ben. "C'mon, if you're coming!"

Ben ran for his hat and was outside in minutes.

The Land Cruiser moved along the dirt road away from the farmhouse when Darius finally spoke. "I'm glad you decided to come today." Ben slanted his eyes in Darius's direction in disbelief. Ben continued to look at Darius from the corner of his eye until Darius said, "No. Really."

"What's with you, man?" Ben asked puzzled. "You act like a wounded dog."

"I'm sorry," Darius managed. "Everyone's a marriage counsellor these days. I'm tired of it."

"Tell them to mind their own business," Ben offered. Darius shot Ben a look of disbelief. "Alright, spill it."

"My father and sister," Darius confessed. "Hell, Carrie has Chris asking why I treat women terrible."

"Relax, Darius. I'm sure the advice was given in good faith."

"I would appreciate if someone could see it from my perspective."

"I understand."

Darius stopped the Land Cruiser and pulled over to the shoulder of the road. He leaned across the steering wheel, his palm supported his chin. Darius sat silently.

"Try to keep an open mind," Ben cajoled. "You tend to be stubborn at times."

Unexpectedly both men started to laugh simultaneously.

Once Darius's disposition improved Ben ventured, "About your sister --"

"What about her?"

"I like her," Ben confessed. "I think she's attracted to me as well."

"Why you old dog!" Darius accused, "That's good news."

"You were right about one thing, Darius."

"What's that?"

"She may straighten me out after all. When I'm with her, I feel this flutter in my stomach," Ben remarked laconically.

"Better watch your step with Carrie," Darius warned.

"What do you mean by that?" Ben questioned incredulously.

Darius laughed, starting the Land Cruiser's engine. "You figure it out!"

~* * * *~

Darius was more distant than ever and Moriah wondered if she should ask him about it. Perhaps Nancy had been a cold woman? Darius mentioned he had travelled a great deal. Maybe the separation caused them marital problems? There were any number of reasons for a divorce. It was not uncommon for a lonely man away from home to seek female companionship. Maybe Darius had a low opinion of women? But why? Perhaps they were unable to communicate? A million possibilities occurred to Moriah.

Why would her husband deny them the opportunity for a real marriage? Moriah was convinced there was a chemistry between them regardless how much Darius resisted. She wanted him to share her hopes, dreams and disappointments. If only Darius would lower his defenses, she could help him overcome his distrust and fears.

Moriah considered that she mulled over the possibilities long enough. She dressed and moved in search of Rebecca. She wanted answers to her questions.

A knock at the door captured Carrie's attention, she moved toward it. Nora Johnson introduced herself as a neighbor and breezed inside.

After Carrie introduced herself, she continued, "This is my mother, Rebecca Mc Coy and my son, Chris," Carrie added.

"Pleased to meet you, Nora," Rebecca said bobbing her head.

"Have a seat, Nora." Carrie gestured to the wicker sofa. When everyone was seated, the sound of approaching footsteps caused them to turn curiously. Moriah entered the living room.

"What a pleasant surprise, Nora," Moriah greeted.

"It has been awhile," Nora began. "I want to invite you and Darius to the dance we're having at the school."

This was the opportunity Moriah sought. A chance to bring their relationship out in the open. Darius's aloofness troubled Moriah and her patience was growing thin. Until now he had been in control. He always avoided any mention of the word commitment. Moriah found this degrading not to mention, puzzling. She vowed she would make him confide in her and admit what troubled him, this was her only hope.

"I would love to," Moriah responded, searching everyone's face. "When is the dance?"

"Wednesday night," Nora invited, her eyes scanning the group's response. "Of course your family is welcome."

"Oh, I don't really think --" Rebecca interjected.

"What mother means is, we would be delighted," Carrie interrupted.

"Great." Nora stood. "I'm sorry to rush off but my kids will be home soon." Moving toward the front door, she added, "Nice meeting everyone. I look forward to seeing you at the dance." Nora remained a few minutes longer giving them directions to the school.

Moriah accompanied her neighbor to the front door.

"What a stroke of luck," Carrie said to herself. With as sigh of satisfaction, she slumped back in the chair.

~* * * *~

Seth located Darius with Jason's help. He turned the motor off and climbed out of Taurus station wagon.

Darius observed his father's approach. He hoped nothing was amiss.

"What are you building son?"

"A gazebo. If we want to picnic by the lake we can be cool and comfortable." Darius furrowed his brows in question.

"Everything is fine. I wanted to get away from the women for awhile." Seth laughed. "How's it coming?"

"Great. I'll have it completed in a couple of days."

"The lake is a pleasant surprise considering this place is hot," Seth commented. "Are you trying to work off some steam from you encounter with Carrie?" Seth grinned.

His father loved to bait him and Darius knew Carrie inherited her tenacity from their father.

"She makes me angrier than anyone."

"I'm sure whatever it was, she didn't mean anything by it."

Darius refused to discuss the matter. This was a private affair and he always handled his own problems. "Want to give me a hand?"

"Got an extra hammer?"

"In the toolbox."

The men talked as they worked.

He recalled the scene at breakfast with Carrie earlier. Darius realized he was the cause of problems in his marriage. For this reason, Carrie's barbs grated on him.

Seth hadn't noticed Ben Willis at first. Ben was busy repairing a fence in the distance. Seth had hoped to find Darius alone and get to the bottom of this. Ben was approaching now. Seth regarded him curiously.

"Hello, Mr. Mc Coy," Ben greeted. He adopted his best smile, Ben sensed the vibes were anything but good.

Seth gave Ben a curt nod, then shifted his attention back to his son. Darius broke the silence.

"Ben you've done a terrific job repairing the fence. Thanks," Darius complimented.

"But it will cost you," Ben teased. Why was Seth Mc Coy's expression serious? Ben had put forth his best efforts to help Darius lighten his mood. Just when he was about to succeed, Seth shows up and undermines Ben's efforts. Who knows why this time? Ben thought.

"Are you sure you want to be a rancher?" Seth interjected. "Looks like a lot of work."

Darius wasn't put off by hard work. "Surely as I chose a career in the army," Darius replied, puzzled.

"What about children?" Seth stopped to wipe his brow with a forearm. "You're not getting any younger."

"You're right." Darius's said sarcastically. "But I will be there while my children are growing up."

Ben rolled his eyes skyward. They were acting like two bucks who locked horns over a territorial dispute. Why were they always at odds? Darius resented Seth's absence when he was growing up. Ben thought Darius had overcome this long ago. Ben ambled to the opposite side of the gazebo to work. This could get dicey momentarily and Ben wanted to be clear of it.

"You sure as hell won't have any children at this rate!" Seth prodded.

First it was Ben, then Carrie, and now his father was sticking his nose into Darius's affairs. Why couldn't they mind their own business? Truth was, Darius married to obtain a son. Grimacing, Darius rallied to the challenge. His eyes engaging Seth's.

"How do you know Moriah's not pregnant?" Darius jeered. Seth's stunned expression pleased him.

"The way you and Carrie were going at it, I considered a man's edgy when he's been celibate to long," Seth hazarded.

"That's not the problem." Darius heaved a frustrated sigh. He did not relish the idea of a confrontation with his father. It was time to keep his cool he rationalized. "C'mon Dad, it's time we stopped for lunch." Seth allowed the subject to drop. Ben moved in their direction, a relieved expression on his face.

When they arrived back at *The Flying M Ranch*, the men wiped their feet before entering the house. The women had lunch prepared and the dining table set formally. What was the occasion? Darius was convinced they were up to mischief and soon the women would lower the boom. Seth was quiet and moved to greet his wife. Smiling Darius addressed everyone, then excused himself to clean up before rejoining them at the table. He knew something was brewing and he would steer clear of it for as long as possible.

Ben was relieved by the short respite. Earlier by the lake he thought a confrontation between the two head-strong men was inevitable. If he could keep them apart perhaps the visit would prove to be pleasant.

During lunch Moriah mentioned Nora's invitation to the dance. This could be an opportunity to meet the neighbors she pointed out. Moriah expressed an interest in making new friends and in community activities. Carrie and Rebecca reinforced Moriah's efforts to persuade the men the dance was a good idea. Darius knew he didn't stand a chance against the women once they were determined. He considered the dance might prove a pleasant distraction for everyone and he might even enjoy it. Alas Darius agreed they should attend the dance. The women were more than pleased when all the men finally agreed. Afterward the women increased their efforts to cater to them by solicitation of extra helpings, coffee and dessert to show their appreciation.

Wednesday night arrived and Moriah was so excited she could barely contain herself. This would be the first social function they attended in Austin area. She felt a strong urge to become a part of the community. She was happier since the Mc Coys arrival. Perhaps their presence would dissolve the barrier Darius built between them. Everyone seemed to like her, except Darius. Moriah failed to understand why he sent for her? Pushing all doubts aside, Moriah slipped into an aquamarine dress for the dance.

The school was alight in the velvety night. Moriah noticed several automobiles and trucks in the parking area as everyone climbed out of the station wagon and started for the dance. Inside the school building colored lights twinkled overhead. Ceiling fans blew the string of lights which created the illusion of fireflies dancing in the moonlight.

"I'm glad you folks could make it," Lamar said. He was amazed the whole family turned out. "I think it will be a lot of fun and give everyone a chance to get acquainted."

The crowd buzzed with conversation. Lamar introduced the Mc Coys to several of the local people, explaining who everyone was in the community of five thousand. It appeared everyone owned a ranch of one size or another. Tonight people of all ages were present and more than congenial. Darius and Moriah were proud to be a part of the community of Sinclair. Darius considered this could prove to be just what their relationship needed to progress.

Moments later a trio began to play a series of sixties music. The Mc Coys joined a large group at the Johnson's table as everyone participated in eager conversation. The oldies brought back wonderful memories for Seth, he explained to

Rebecca as he led her onto the dance floor. Others soon followed suit and were dancing and laughing.

Carrie said, "Nora, I'm glad your babysitter didn't mind watching Chris tonight."

The two women were getting on famously, Moriah thought looking around the room.

Drumming his fingers on the tabletop, Darius was pleased he had come. Impressive job decorating the cafeteria he considered.

Seth tapped Darius's arm and whispered, "Ask your wife to dance."

He gazed in Moriah's direction. A faint smile covered her face as she scanned the room. Darius stood and extended his hand to her.

"May I have this dance?" She rose and moved into his arms. An appreciative gleam in his eyes, he drew her close. Moriah hadn't realized how much she craved his touch.

"You feel good in my arms," Darius said. Moriah snuggled her cheek into his shirt, inhaling the musk scent.

"Are you glad you decided to come?" Moriah questioned.

"Very much."

Lamar nudged Seth to one side. "Everyone could loosen up some. What do you say, we spike the punch?"

Seth chuckled, "With what?" Lamar removed a small flask from his jacket. Seth pointed out, "Beer and wine are offered." Lamar shook his head. Seth and Lamar volunteered to refresh everyone's drinks and moved toward the punch bowl after gathering the requests.

Seth blocked Lamar from view while he emptied the flask's contents into the punch bowl. Seth's eyes grew wide. Being naughty caused them to lift their brows expectantly. Presently the song ended and another began. The two men smiled as they poured punch for everyone and returned to the Johnson table distributing the drinks.

Darius enjoyed holding Moriah as they moved sensuously to the slow tune. Moriah looked up, smiling. Their body language spoke volumes he thought. She seemed to enjoy being his arms or so he thought, Darius pulled her closer.

Carrie and Nora were huddled together whispering. Rebecca was bobbing her head in rhythm with the music. The place was alight with laugher and good will.

"Want to dance, Becky?" Seth asked.

"I thought you'd never ask," Rebecca drawled, accepting the glass of punch. She took a sip and stood.

"Can't live without me?"

"You flatter yourself."

"That's what I like most about you," Seth teased as they arrived on the dance floor. "Your sense of humor." Rebecca shifted her eyes upward, as if expecting divine intervention. Seth noticed Darius and Moriah dancing as though they were the only ones in the room.

"That's more like it," Seth said softly. Rebecca's eyes followed his. Smiling she nodded in agreement.

Ben looked forward to the idea of attending the dance from the moment it was mentioned. Grinning he approached Carrie. Carrie pivoted slightly in her chair as she watched his approach. Carrie's eyes were flirtatious in their assessing gaze. Ben suspected she liked what she saw. She had a sense of mischief in her bearing, he appreciated her vivaciousness. The black dress she wore was feline he thought. Ben considered himself the gambling kind, he would give her a whirl.

Trepidation filled Carrie for once, she was speechless. She smiled as she accepted his hand. She hoped the drumbeat in her ears would stop. What was wrong with her? Carrie moved into Ben's arms.

Ben had trouble describing the way he felt - oh perhaps, like a big goose bump! He laughed in an attempt to maintain their distance. Both would be amazed if they could see their faces at this moment. There was definite chemistry between them and this, they recognized.

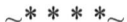

~* * * *~

CHAPTER 10

Darius could not ignore the slow fire that spread through him. He and Moriah fit together like integral parts of a puzzle. Could she feel him tremble? Moriah lifted her head, gazing seductively into his eyes.

Accordingly the slow song ended and they withdrew. It was a terrible time for his hormones to take over Darius thought. Her eyes were cloudy darkened pools filled with a warmth that washed over him. He wanted to be alone with Moriah.

Darius crossed the room with her in tow. "Please, wait here." Approaching Seth on the dance floor, he briefly whispered something in his father's ear before he returned to Moriah's side.

"Let's get some air." He did not allow her time to respond. Clasping her hand in his, Darius led Moriah toward the door.

Outside the air was warm on this starry night with barely a quarter moon peering through the clouds. His determined stride puzzled Moriah.

"Where are you taking me?"

"You'll see."

The narrow pathway behind the school yard led to a dark overgrown area. Two-by-fours jutted overhead covered with verdant flora, fauna and hanging gourds. A gravel walkway led in several directions. Encircling them a maze of plants grew together climbing upward wrapping themselves around the beams overhead sealing the enclosure on all sides. The crunch of gravel sounded under their feet as they walked.

"What is this?"

"Somewhere we can be alone."

"But it's so dark."

"Are you afraid?"

"No. Must we go so far?"

Darius stacked wooden boxes together he found in the alcove seats. He tested them for sturdiness. "Sit here." Moriah stared at the makeshift seat and blinked. "They will support us."

Carefully she sat down on the wooden boxes. He followed suit.

"Why the secrecy?"

"This." Darius grasped her upper arms hauling her to him as he angled his mouth over hers. He savored her honey sweetness, her pouty lips, her softness. He could not remember when last he indulged in spontaneity.

Moriah threw her head back, exposing her neck to his warm moist lips. With a groan, he moved to her cheek then trailed kisses along her neck. "You're skin is so soft." He returned to her mouth once more. His tongue solicited entry into her warm recess. Moriah's lips parted, his tongue darted in feverishly. She returned his kiss and movements with equal effort.

Darius felt as if his body suddenly melted into hers. He could not get close enough. With each suggestive thrust of his tongue, she returned one of her own. Darius's pulse drummed in his ears.

Moriah gasped for breath when he ran the tip of his tongue along one breast. Her hand moved from his shoulder to cup the crown of his head pulling him closer yet. Surely he has some feelings for her or he wouldn't behave this way? Moriah could not think, just feel.

Damn! Why did his traitorous body choose now of all times? Darius wondered. This insatiable hunger would not be mollified. Both submitted to the urgent need.

He continued to caress her pliant body. His heart slammed against his chest as a liquid warmth washed over him. Darius unzipped her dress, pushing it urgently over her shoulders. His lips followed the path set forth, kissing her shoulders, Moriah trembled in his embrace.

Misinterpreting her reaction, Darius abruptly dropped both arms to his sides, his fists clenching as he withdrew and turned away. Darius was unprepared for the emotions she elicited. This angered him. He didn't need anyone he told himself. It had proven unwise in the past. "I'm sorry. You must think me an animal."

She struggled for a moment to comprehend the myriad of emotions that overwhelmed her. She knew Darius shared the excitement earlier. She had not imagined this, Darius was reaching out to her. She had trouble understanding what happened. Preening herself, Moriah considered him an enigma. One minute they were making love, the next she didn't know what to think.

"I am your wife."

Darius turned to face her. "But there's a time and a place for things."

Anger grew inside her like never before. Moriah was convinced she missed some of the conversation somewhere.

Well, she'd had enough of the verbal sparring and this nonsense. Maybe Carrie was correct? Perhaps she had a great deal to learn of men? Despite his rejection Moriah would not allow him to regard her as a possession. She deserved better. This would stop and stop, now!

"Oh, really?" Moriah snapped. "And when will that be?"

Surely his ears deceived him? Darius remained rooted to the spot, silent. Moriah saw several emotions cross his face -- disbelief, frustration, and disgust. Given this he regained his composure and resolved himself to the situation at hand, she was angry. The tone of her voice was it sarcasm?

He had handled delicate situations before. Hell if anyone should be angry he reasoned, it would be him. His body still throbbed with need. All at once Darius realized how insensitive and selfish he'd been. He had wanted to take her right here, he cursed himself for it.

"You're angry?"

She stared at him in disbelief. "I think that's obvious." Moriah sighed in exasperation. "Until now Darius, you have toyed with me when it suits you," she began. "I resent you for it. I have needs like other women, yet you turn me away. Why?"

Darius uttered an expletive under his breath.

"Why won't you confide in me?" When no response was forthcoming, she hazarded, "I won't have you regard me as a possession, to toss me aside whenever you tire of the novelty." The frustration in her voice was more than apparent.

His eyes narrowed to slits. A muscle twitched along Darius's jaw. "You knew the terms of the agreement before coming to America," he ground out.

"That's not the issue here," Moriah interrupted, "and you know it." Moriah took two deep breaths in an effort to calm herself. "You're chauvinistic," she accused. Darius looked as if someone had thrown cold water in his face.

"Chauvinistic?" After taking several deep breaths, he spoke the word as if he had heard it for the first time.

"Exactly."

He remained silent, his gaze assessing her.

"If you don't know, I cannot explain it to you." Her voice was low and clipped as she strode past him, leaving him to stare after her.

Moriah was incensed. Her emotions had plummeted skyward only to be deflated. A tear fell to her cheek as she went inside to join the others.

Darius stood for a moment trying to decide what happened. He ploughed a hand through his hair, then cupped his chin in one hand. Women! They were all the same -- impossible! If he hadn't longed for a son, damn it, he would have remained a bachelor. Slowly he walked back to the dance.

Grabbing a long neck beer, Darius took a large drink from the bottle. His eyes travelled to Moriah. By this time she had rejoined Carrie, Nora and Ben at their table. From the smile on her face she was enjoying the conversation. Darius heard Lamar telling one of his tall tales, and everyone was having fun, except him.

What was wrong with him? Darius wondered. He'd never experienced such mixed feelings. He recognized lust moments ago -- he was not confused about that. What bewildered him were his emotions toward his wife. He enjoyed her company yet her lack of spirit at times grated on him. Seemingly this was changing, she surprised him when she stood her ground tonight. Was Moriah a threat to his self-declared supremacy? Darius pushed the thoughts aside. He finished the beer and took another. He remained detached, he needed time to sort this out.

Carrie pretended she hadn't noticed her brother standing near the refreshment table. Darius's frustration was more than evident and the way he continued to nurse one beer after another.

She turned away to answer something her mother asked and when she turned back he was gone. Why had Darius not rejoined the group? Moriah seemed untouched by Darius's behavior. Carrie wondered if she ever lost control.

Lamar continued to entertain everyone with his jokes. Moriah laughed until her sides hurt. She needed a distraction because her mind was racing and she was thoroughly confused and angry.

Carrie feigned interest in the conversation, actually her mind was elsewhere. Her thoughts were focused on teaching Moriah to become an American woman. Carrie heard oriental women adapted easily to Western ideas. When she was finished with Moriah, Darius's orderly life would be uprooted.

Darius's detachment kept him from caring for anyone - it was his shield against injury. He was an emotional coward, Carrie considered. She wanted him to be happy and to start living again. She needed help and this was where Nora fit into the picture. Truth was she was almost certain her plan would work.

Moriah was smiling on the outside, inwardly she was humiliated by Darius's behavior. Why was he inconsiderate of her feelings? Why hadn't he returned to the party? Instead he remained by the doorway with a faraway look. Now, he was nowhere to be found. Seth's perceptiveness came to the rescue, he asked Moriah to dance.

After three or four glasses of punch, Moriah forgot her problems. Tonight she desperately needed to get out of the house. She wanted to be appreciated for herself. Why Darius failed to understand this was beyond her imagination.

When the dance was over, Seth apologized for his son. He explained domestic quarrels sometimes happen. His son simply had too much to drink. Nora and Lamar expressed their delight at meeting everyone and bid them goodnight.

When the Mc Coys approached the station wagon, Seth saw Darius sprawled in the back seat, asleep. Damn, him! Seth thought. Despite close family ties, Darius was always a loner. The boy had an independent streak. Why was he behaving this way? Seth wondered.

Carrie noticed the way Moriah ignored Darius. This was just the beginning Darius, Carrie chuckled to herself gazing at her brother passed out in the back seat.

When they returned to the ranch Seth deliberately brought the automobile to an abrupt stop. Indolently, Darius lifted his head for the first time and looked around. He was blitzed. Seth decided to wait until morning to speak with him. Everyone climbed from the station wagon and moved in the direction of the farmhouse. Disgusted, Moriah left her husband to fend for himself. Darius was the last to exit the automobile. Attempting some dignity, he struggled to walk without stumbling. Seth remained in the living room after everyone retired that night. Darius entered the house when Seth began the onslaught.

"The least you could have done was to be a gentleman and remain at the dance," Seth began warming to the conversation. "But no, you disregarded everyone's feelings for your own."

"What the hell?" Darius said sluggishly.

"What are you trying to prove?"

"That's really none of your affair."

"It may not be, but I think you've been callous toward your wife," Seth accused. His anger grew by the moment.

"As far as my lack of consideration --" Darius gave a disgruntled snort. His bleary eyes, now flashing.

"Now that you mention it," Seth interrupted, "Let's discuss that point."

"I've seen the looks you've given me all night." With each word Darius's voice rose an octave. "I don't need anyone to apologize for me."

"What?"

"I heard the excuses you made in my behalf. My personal life is my business!"

"Whether or not you like it, I think you've been a schmuck."

"I suppose you never have?" Darius sneered.

"So you admit it?"

"No." Darius struggled to collect his thoughts. He didn't want Seth's advice nor to hear his displeasure. Darius had enough problems without the intrusion. Tonight he allowed his chaotic emotions to cloud his judgment. He tried to express them to Moriah the only way he knew how -- by making love to her. Truth was, lately he held Moriah at distance and was beginning to regret it. Darius expected her to be warm and inviting. Her rejection had blown him away. He didn't handle rejection well. This incident brought back the painful memories. Uncertain of how to react to Moriah, he resorted to old habits -- hiding his emotions.

"What's the matter, boy?" Seth's sarcasm brought Darius out of himself.

"In case you haven't noticed, I'm a man." Darius gave a deep sigh, his anger more than evident. "To answer your question, not a damn thing I can't handle."

"You have a funny way of showing it," Seth paused, his expression chagrined. For a moment Darius glared at Seth, turning away he released a sound of pure disgust.

"Moriah is sweet and she waits on your every whim and you treat her like . . . well, you neglect her."

"That's between Moriah and me," Darius said in a chilly tone. He resented Seth's interference. Darius cursed himself for the grudge he held. "You're a hell of an example," he said brusquely.

Seth recognized the stubborn look. Darius inherited his major flaw he considered.

The odd expression on Seth's face did not deter him. Old resentments die hard, Darius thought. "What about your lack of concern for your family? For Mom?" he shouted.

"What are you trying to say?" Seth challenged, his eyes engaging his son's.

"What about the times you weren't around when Carrie and I were growing up? The times you left Mom alone? She always made excuses for you. Damn it, anyway! You cared more for your blasted career than for your family!"

"That's not true. It was my duty as an officer." Seth paused before speaking again. "You never forgave me." Now Seth's voice was a little more than a whisper.

"It doesn't matter anymore. Just don't try to tell me how to handle my life or my marriage." Darius turned and left Seth standing alone.

Fury grew inside him with each step he took toward the bedroom. Darius halted outside their bedroom door. He heard the door close quietly behind Seth as he entered the guest room. He also noticed the lights went out shortly after Seth entered their room. Darius remained rooted to the spot for a few moments as he heard muffled voices in his parent's room briefly, then silence.

What did Moriah say to everyone when she rejoined the group? It was unlike his father to attack him. He deliberated a moment then swayed in his stance. What the hell! She was his wife and it was time she knew it. His body still ached with need. He opened the door and moved inside and crossed over to the bed. He could hear water running in the shower. He undressed and moved toward the sound.

He saw her outline clearly through the glass door. Quietly he slipped inside. Moriah released a startled gasp stepping back against the wall. Intent on feeling the water pelt his skin, he closed his eyes instinctively as he lowered his head under the nozzle. Darius let the water run over his head and shoulders, then wiped the beads of water from his face and opened his eyes.

He had never seen such perfection, but Moriah was even more beautiful than he imagined.

"What are you doing here?" she managed.

"I think that's obvious." The determined glint in his eyes indicated he expected her to comply.

Surely he wouldn't? Or would he?

"You know what I mean." His lips compressed, the smile did not reach his eyes. "This is the time and place."

Moriah's expression perplexed him. What was with her? One minute she acts angry because he hadn't taken her and when he decides to accommodate her, she reacts in a frightened manner. Darius shook his head in dismay. What would it take for them to be on the same channel? At the same time?

Perhaps Moriah found the chase more stimulating than the catch he considered. Darius never prized things that came easily to him. The shower sobered him. With a wolfish grin, Darius reached out for her. He drew Moriah to him, tilted his head and took her mouth in a feral kiss.

There was no doubt about his strength, virility or what was on his mind. He held her with minimal effort, oblivious to her rejection. Fear overcame her, Moriah moved her hands from their flattened position on his chest to push him away. Adopting her best indignant look, she steeled herself for his next move. The best way to deal with an opponent was never to show fear. Instinctively, Moriah released a disgusted sound from her throat.

Even in his present state, it was clear from his expression he had not anticipated her response. He pulled back.

She took a tentative step back. It's only a respite she told herself. Guarding against further attempts, Moriah snapped, "What do you want?"

"To make love to my wife." His irritated expression indicated he thought she was dense.

"What makes you think you can push your way in here?" Moriah demanded.

"This is my home. And as I said before, you're my wife." Darius's voice was brusque. "Come here."

Moriah considered if he thought proving his manhood was what she wanted, he had better think again. In the present state, he was anything but appealing. She would rather die before enduring his drunken lovemaking. "No."

Ignoring her refusal, he reached out for her. Try as she might, Moriah was trapped. She had never known him to be demanding, arrogant and cold. His eyes held no emotion. Moriah panicked and struggled to hold back the tears, she took a deep breath, and pushed him away, hard. The contempt on her face must have convinced him. For a moment disbelief flickered briefly in his eyes, then he released her.

"You refuse me?" His insolence made Moriah want to slap him and wipe the imperious look off his face.

"I dislike the thought of your touch." The words were out before she could think.

"You didn't find me so objectionable before," he snarled.

"And you weren't acting like an animal," Moriah retorted. "Now, get out!"

For a moment his eyes reflected hurt, then his expression hardened. "You won't have to endure my attentions further." He strode out of the bathroom, retrieved his clothes and quietly shut the door behind him.

The deadly tone of his voice alerted Moriah her words hit their mark. She did not care for the way he acted as if any woman would do.

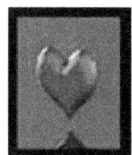

CHAPTER 11

"You look like the day after the storm," Carrie taunted.

"You missed your calling. Maybe you should have been a comedian?" Darius said blandly, buttoning his shirt as the coffeemaker began to fill.

"It must have been a wild night."

"You're not starting on me too?"

"Only because you're hung over after last night," Carrie admitted wryly.

Darius felt like hell alright. Last night he had made a schmuck of himself. Damn! There was no rationale behind his behavior either Darius told himself.

"Thanks for the reminder," he ground out. "My head is pounding."

Carrie reached inside a cupboard and withdrew a bottle of aspirin. "Just so you can't say I am heartless, here." She held out two tablets in her palm. Darius accepted them.

"Breakfast?"

"Ple-ease!" He drew the word out as he darted her a sideways look. He was in no mood for Carrie's antics. Darius had a quick cup of coffee then started for the door.

He gunned the Land Cruiser's engine and drove away. Today he would finish the gazebo. He could blame his ill feelings on the liquor but he knew better. As a drunken fool he had pushed his way into the bedroom and he had been primed and ready. He didn't blame Moriah for ordering him out. She surprised him by her reaction to his advances. She must be calling him all sorts of names. Probably none he had not thought of already.

Her eyes closed, Moriah stretched as she sat up in bed. Recalling the incident with Darius last night she grimaced. If this was the way beer affected him, perhaps he should watch his intake she considered. She had not enjoyed the incident in the least. Moments later she dressed then went in search of Darius. They must discuss what happened last night she thought.

Carrie greeted her nonchalantly in the kitchen.

"Has Darius come down?" Moriah queried.

"He had his coffee on the run. He left about twenty minutes ago," Carrie responded.

"Did he say anything?"

"Not a word. I don't think he was in a good mood," Carrie replied. "Incidentally Ben and I are going for a ride this afternoon."

"Oh really? Where is Ben?"

"We decided this last night at the dance," Carrie supplied. "He's not a morning person." Her face colored. Moriah looked puzzled for a moment.

"He's sleeping-in today," Carrie supplied.

"You seem to be hitting it off with Ben."

"Yes, I agree," Carrie admitted happily. "It's been a long time. I never thought I would find another man attractive," she mused.

"Ben is a good man," Moriah commented. "He expresses himself openly."

Carrie tilted her head sideways and looked at Moriah from the corner of her eye. She reminded Moriah of Darius. He would look at her with the same shrewd gaze.

"Well he enjoys life and doesn't keep things bottled inside," Moriah commented.

"And you wonder why Darius can't be more like him?"

"Yes," Moriah admitted.

"Darius has been like this since childhood," Carrie explained. "It seems worse since his divorce from Nancy."

Carrie's thoughtful expression perplexed Moriah. "Are you becoming involved with Ben?"

"There's an attraction and we enjoy one another's company," Carrie offered. "When we leave I doubt, I'll ever see him again." Carrie prayed she was wrong.

Carrie's words unexpectedly grew faint. A part of Moriah was relieved Darius had gone. Another part wanted to confront him about his behavior. Moriah disliked the manner in which he made his intentions clear he wanted a son. She had hoped he would grow to appreciate her, to love her. For all he cared she might as well be a salmon travelling upstream to spawn.

"Why are you so pale?" Carrie asked in amazement.

Moriah shook herself mentally.

"Are you ill?"

"No. Upset." Moriah settled into her cup of coffee.

"About what?"

"Your brother."

"Oh that!" Carrie dismissed this as an everyday occurrence. "What has he done now?"

"He doesn't regard me as his wife. I'm merely a warm body to bear him children," Moriah confessed. She could not help it, Darius humiliated her. "It seems, I'm not worthy of respect or consideration."

"You're finally tired of it?"

"I'm uncertain what to do about it." Moriah knew she shouldn't involve Carrie in their domestic problems but she had nowhere to turn. She was acquainted with Nora, but personal matters should remain within the family.

"I have a plan." Carrie began to explain her plan to Moriah. She moved closer to listen tentatively.

"We'll transform you into an American woman."

"How do you propose to do this?"

"My brother is used to you being subservient and submissive."

"You're saying I should be disagreeable?"

"Not exactly." She would be a role model for Moriah.

Carrie paused a moment in thought. Concern for her brother's happiness overwhelmed her. Darius could be stubborn at times. She would have to work fast. Drastic times call for desperate measures. Carrie would not allow him to lose heart; to forsake love. She cared for him to much. Darius refused to trust women since the divorce. She considered he had a few timely lessons to learn about women. And Carrie decided she was the one to do it.

"You'll need outside interests. Propriety dictates one must do things in an acceptable manner.

"When there are decisions to be made, Darius likes to be consulted. He won't like this," Moriah explained.

"That's what I am counting on. He has lived in rarefied air for a long time. He likes everyone at his beckon call -- especially women." His treatment of Moriah grated on Carrie.

She was cognizant their father influenced Darius's opinions of women but Carrie would change this. She refused to allow him to lose his one real chance for happiness.

"Tell me about Darius's relationship with Nancy?" Moriah questioned anxiously. She had to know.

Carrie frowned. "Why?"

"He's been hurt badly, I can feel it. He will not allow us to become close," Moriah regretfully admitted.

"You mean he hasn't consummated the marriage?" Carrie couldn't suppress her laughter. "This is better than I thought."

"It's not like that." Moriah disliked speaking of intimate matters, but she refused to allow Carrie the wrong impression.

Carrie stopped laughing. "We'll give him a dose of his own medicine."

"But you'll be here only a few more days," Moriah reasoned.

"That's where Nora comes in."

"Oh, you didn't?"

"I only mentioned what she needs to know," Carrie reassured.

"Do you think it will work?"

"With some coaching anything is possible."

~* * * *~

Darius knew his behavior the night before was abominable. Years of suppressed anger suddenly overwhelmed him. Release surely at hand, it burst forth like a caged animal. He disliked sharing Moriah with anyone. The short time they were together, he found he enjoyed having her around, tending him. He hadn't realized how lonely and possessive he had become. He had allowed painful memories to burden him - it still hurt to be unworthy of love.

He drove to the farmhouse near the noon hour. He had contemplated the situation until his head screamed for relief. He regretted most of his behavior last night, particularly with Moriah. He had never tried to force his attentions on a woman before. The thought never occurred she might refuse him. What a fat-headed fool he was!

The hang-over he suffered was bad enough but the question of how to deal with Moriah was a real problem. Seth and Jason were playing with the pups when he drove into the yard.

"It won't be long, they'll be eating the house down," Jason said scratching Max, the English sheep dog's ear. Both men agreed Max might scare an intruder by his sheer size provided he didn't lick them to death first.

"I see you're jealous Murphy," Seth spoke to the Springer Spaniel nudging him for his share of the attention. Both men turned to the sound of an approaching vehicle.

Darius stepped out of the Land Cruiser and pushed the door shut, approaching Jason and Seth.

He gave a half nod. "Jason. Dad, how's it going?" He squatted to pet the puppies.

"Quiet," Jason said. "I've put away the supplies in the barn. And that new calf is growing, it's all legs."

"That's good." Darius dodged the wet tongue that swept out to meet him. He chuckled at the puppies.

"Did you finish the gazebo?" Seth inquired since Darius seemed in better disposition.

"Not entirely." Both dogs began to bark.

"C'mon boys, I'll fix your vittles," Jason drawled. The puppies followed closely at Jason's heels as he started for the barn.

Moriah watched both men through the window. Darius's serious demeanor fired her curiosity. What were they discussing? What would she say to him? How would he regard her?

Carrie's plan was foolish. It would never work.

Fifteen minutes later, Darius and Seth entered the house. They appeared in good spirits Moriah thought watching them take a seat at the table.

"Jason and Grandpa took me to see the calf, mommy. You should see it," Chris said in excitement. "Uncle Darius has a lot of cows."

"I would like to see them," Carrie conceded.

"How was your day, Darius?" Moriah asked. Until now he avoided meeting her gaze -- the coward, she thought. He lifted his eyes to hers.

"I can't complain," Darius remarked light-heartedly, returning to his meal.

Moriah bit her tongue. She wanted to stomp his foot to gain his attention. Each time she tried to pin him down he managed to dodge the issue. Moriah was displeased to say the least. And to think he'd been unaffected by his actions last night infuriated her.

"The food, is it alright?" Moriah deliberately shifted her gaze to Darius. Everyone gave a quizzical look. The atmosphere wreaked with tension.

Darius looked up from his plate. "What's this about, Moriah?" He gave her a measured look warning her to remain silent.

Carrie tried to start a conversation. "It's wonderful of you Moriah to help Nora with the project for the Women's Club." Of course Darius wouldn't make this easy, she thought. "The new wing for the school will be a real asset."

"Moriah, you really should meet some of the women in the area," Rebecca said in agreement. "It's a worthy cause. In addition it's a good way to be apprised of the community's needs and become involved."

Darius was relieved the conversation shifted to a neutral subject. When no one watched, Moriah's inquisitive eyes asked silent questions of him. He was not prepared to deal with them now. He was struggling with his own feelings of confusion, shame, apprehension and disgust. Unfamiliar emotions assailed him he could not define. He barely heard any of the conversation at the table.

Carrie noticed her brother never said a word in response to hearing Moriah would become involved outside the home. He was enmeshed in his own thoughts she mused.

Moriah tried to draw him out but he was indifferent. She was relieved he had the grace to look remorseful when their eyes met briefly. Nevertheless Moriah was deflated.

When asked what he thought of Moriah's involvement with the Women's Club, Darius agreed this would benefit her. He felt like a Class-A-Number-One-Heel. Darius wanted to speak to her however he would wait until tonight when they were alone. The distressed look on Moriah's face was almost more than he could bear.

Everyone was more than aware of the tension in the room. They spoke of general subjects like the weather to fill the silent void. After lunch Darius and Seth left to finish the gazebo.

~* * * *~

CHAPTER 12

"He didn't take the bait. I can't believe it," Carrie said in amazement after Rebecca left the room to lay Chris down for a nap.

"I don't think he likes me," Moriah admitted.

"Don't be silly of course he likes you. You're his wife," Carrie corrected.

"No. He wants a son. He does not care what he must do to achieve this. A wife is unimportant." Moriah's heart ached. She had been a fool for hoping he might grow to love her. He made no pretense of his motives a tiny voice within her supplied. How would she deal with the situation? Carrie explained where Nora fit into the plan. Moriah listened with renewed interest.

~* * *~

"Why is Darius being difficult?" Carrie asked Ben after they rode out a distance on the horses away from the farmhouse.

"I didn't come out here to discuss Darius," Ben remarked. "I prefer to learn more about you." He grinned.

Carrie gave him a knowing grin. "It's off limits, huh?" Ben nodded. "Okay."

"Right over there should be a fine place for a picnic," Ben pointed out.

They dismounted and tethered the horses. Ben wanted to make sure he found a place where they could be alone. Their allotted time together was short and Ben really liked Carrie. Thank goodness, she was unlike her brother. Virgo males were normally to intense to suit Ben. The only reason he and Darius remained friends was due to Darius's honesty and loyalty. A deep trust bonded them. Given this, Ben was only interested in pursuing Carrie at the moment.

They spread a blanket and laid out the supplies for the picnic.

"You looked great last night," Ben said.

"And I don't, now?"

Ben rolled his eyes at Carrie.

"I couldn't resist," Carrie supplied.

"You have a quick-wit, Carrie. I prefer intelligent women."

"Why are you complaining?"

"You're making this difficult," Ben explained.

"I am? How?" Carrie gave Ben an innocent, puzzled expression.

"Leave it to me to find my equal."

"I have a feeling there's a compliment hidden in there somewhere."

"There is, in a way. But, there's also a problem," Ben added.

Carrie remained silent.

"You make me laugh. It's hard to be romantic when you're laughing."

"You have a point there. What's your intention? Did you bring me out here to seduce me?"

Ben released an exasperated sigh, Carrie's directness caught him off guard. This could restrict their relationship he thought.

"I'm sorry, Ben," Carrie said apologetically. "This is all new to me. I feel awkward."

"There's no reason to be Carrie," Ben said softly. "You must not feel guilty we're attracted. I'd like to spend as much time as possible with you."

Carrie was moved by Ben's honesty and his apparent interest in her. Most men found her intimidating. What a relief to find someone who appreciated her intelligence.

"I must admit, I'm surprised. I never thought I would find another man attractive."

"Why would you think that?" Ben asked incredulously. "You are young, attractive, intelligent, charming -- like me."

"Now, who's being a fat-head?"

Ben realized he'd better instill a bit of seriousness, otherwise he would never get anywhere with Carrie. "Let's toast to our new friendship," Ben said popping the cork of the bottle of wine he had the foresight to bring.

"Well said," Carrie agreed, holding her glass for him to fill.

He liked the way Carrie's face brightened when she smiled. Her mischievous nature eluded him. Ben appreciated Carrie's spunk.

"Tell me about yourself, Ben."

"I grew up an orphan."

"How terrible for you."

"I consider myself lucky," Ben added. "I had great foster parents. It could have been worse."

"You have a great attitude about it."

"No point in bitterness, it eats away at you."

Carrie nodded in acknowledgement.

"Then I met Darius and we've been close from the start. Our relationship has spanned twenty-nine years. I feel we're brothers."

"I hope you don't think of me as a sister," Carrie hazarded.

Ben threw back his head and laughed wholeheartedly. "I think of you, ah, no. I wouldn't describe it that way."

Carrie wanted to hear more.

"How would you describe it?" she prodded.

"Anything but sisterly."

"If you keep this up, we'll never get anywhere." She gave Ben a look of mocked disapproval.

"Don't be insecure."

"I'm not," Carrie said as Ben edged closer. She wasn't as laid back as she appeared. Carrie was nervous, a man hadn't flirted with her in a long time. She was inexperienced.

When he clasped her hand Ben noticed she was trembling. She's just as nervous he thought. Ben leaned into Carrie.

At first his lips brushed hers, testing, allowing her time to withdraw. When she held firm, Ben took this as a green light. He moved into a position where his head was cradled in her lap, he pulled Carrie to him.

Carrie's head was spinning. She thought she had gone to heaven. He felt so good. Ben made her feel beautiful and desirable. Something Carrie had not experienced in a long time. Ben awakened a part of her that had been dormant too long.

When he withdrew, Ben's eyes were tender as he appraised her reaction. Hers were misty he noticed. "I've wondered what it would feel like to kiss you," Ben said.

"And?"

"I was right."

"You were?"

"You ask a lot of questions."

A grin spread across Carrie's face. "I'm a scientist," she pointed out.

"I appreciate your spirit." Ben had no plans of telling her how affected he was by the kiss. Instead of the friendly repartee they shared, he yearned to crush her to him.

"Great. Let's eat, I'm starved," Carrie remarked.

She always managed to unsettle him Ben thought. What intrigued him most about Carrie? She was not particularly beautiful, not to say she was hard to look at, no. He had dated women who were better looking. Yet she possessed an inner beauty, a quick-wit and charm, Ben found lacking in other women. If he wasn't careful matters could easily become unmanageable.

"Tell me about West Point," Carrie suggested.

"I can think of other things, I prefer to talk about," he explained.

"Such as?"

"What's your favorite food?"

"I love Chinese."

"How did you guess?" Ben added. Both laughed.

"Will you join me in another glass of wine?" Carrie coaxed.

She enjoyed Ben's company a great deal and soon he would be leaving. Carrie hoped he would stay in touch with her. What were her expectations? She asked herself. The whole thing was silly. Whereas Ben was stationed at Fort Bragg in North Carolina, she lived in Arizona. Carrie knew long distance romances never worked. Nevertheless, she would enjoy it for the present. He awakened a part of Carrie that made her feel alive as a woman.

Carrie had a faraway look in her eyes Ben observed.

"Do you miss having a man in your life, Carrie?"

"What makes you sure there's not?"

"Answer my question."

"I didn't think so, until now," Carrie admitted. "I've been so busy with my parents and my son. Actually it's taken up a lot of my time." She heaved a relieved sigh. "How did you know?"

"The way you kissed me."

"That bad, huh?"

"Not exactly." Ben pushed an errant sandy lock of hair from Carrie's view. "More like a woman who should be kissed and often."

"Ben don't be confused by a kiss. I'm not an easy mark or desperate," Carrie warned.

"Don't be defensive," Ben said softly.

When he spoke in that tone Carrie could listen to him forever. Each word was like a soft caress, telling her she was desirable. Why couldn't they stay this way forever? Carrie wondered.

Why hadn't Darius mentioned him before she wondered? "How shall I be?"

"Beautiful and desirable." He responded just before his lips claimed hers once more.

~* * * *~

Later than evening when everyone had retired, Darius thought now was an opportune time to speak with his wife. He rapped lightly on their bedroom door.

Moriah swung it open, yet blocked his entry.

"We have to talk."

She lifted her brows in question.

"Either I come inside or we discuss our love life in the hallway," Darius threatened when she did not respond. She stepped back to allow him entry, then closed the door.

"To what, do I owe the honor of your presence?" Moriah said sardonically.

He heaved a deep sigh. She had a right to be angry, he conceded. Darius lowered himself in a chair.

"I don't see that we have anything further to discuss." Moriah hadn't realized the depth of her pain. She wanted to hurt him as much as he hurt her.

"Sit down and listen."

Caught off guard, she obeyed.

"About last night," Darius began. He paused to collect his thoughts. He wanted to find the right words. He had carefully considered the matter all day. Now his rehearsed speech failed him. "I want to apologize for my conduct last night. I was drunk. Otherwise I would never ..."

His statement hurt more than if he hadn't uttered a word, Moriah thought. He was ashamed he desired her and this troubled Moriah.

He was making a mess of this, he thought. "I want you to know how I feel about you."

"I know, how you feel."

"And how is that?" Darius growled.

"You want me at your beckon call. Also you lack regard for my feelings."

"That's not true."

"Oh, really?" Moriah was warming to the argument. "You don't really care about me." He stood in silence.

Abruptly his expression changed from anger to shock. The realization shook him. In order to protect himself against emotional risk, Darius hadn't considered Moriah's feelings.

"I'll admit I have been distant. But you're wrong on one account. I do care for you." Darius advanced on her, clutching her shoulder with one hand, his eyes implored her to listen.

Moriah's resolve weakened. "But last night ..."

"I should never have," he paused. Guilt overcame him. "I would never have ..."

Misinterpreting his words, Moriah was hurt. She was disappointed it displeased him that he desired her. She turned her back to him and said softly, "Please leave."

~****~

CHAPTER 13

Darius wondered if Moriah realized how difficult it was for him to admit he was wrong? He'd never apologized for his actions. Just when he thought he was beginning to understand women, they never failed to amaze him. Somehow he doubted she understood for lack of anything else to say, he quietly left the room.

The next three days passed uneventfully. Darius avoided her like the plague and Moriah refused to acknowledge him except in passing. Thank heaven his family would leave today. It was not as though Moriah disliked them, quite the contrary. The Mc Coys were warm outspoken people, whereas Darius was more reserved. Were it not for his resemblance to Rebecca, Moriah was convinced they switched babies on the Mc Coys in the hospital. Darius was unlike them.

Moriah considered this a problem she would deal with later. Ben left with the Mc Coys Sunday afternoon since his family agreed to drop him at the airport on their way home. After everyone left, the house was quiet. Now they would have to deal directly with one another with no one to intervene. Darius settled back on the wicker sofa in the living room with a glass of tea. His feet were propped on the coffee table Moriah noticed closing the front door.

"You have a nice family," Moriah commented.

"They liked you," he said casually.

If only Darius did.

She took a seat beside him. "Darius tell me about Nancy?"

He gazed up quizzically.

"Did she betray you?"

"What gave you that idea?"

"I want to know why, you don't trust me."

"My relationship with Nancy has nothing to do with us," Darius remarked in a chilly tone. His stern expression indicated he refused to elaborate. "As far as trust, I'm not sure I know what you mean."

"If you refuse to confide in me, how do you expect our relationship to develop?"

"That's where you lose me."

"You want a family and all this." Moriah gestured with a wave of her hand to encompass the house and ranch. "Relationships are built on trust."

"What's all this talk of trust?" Darius asked in amazement. "Have I neglected to fulfil your expectations?" he challenged.

Ignoring his evasiveness she forged ahead. "I realize we were strangers when we married," she said softly. "Each of us entered the marriage for different reasons. You wanted offspring." She bit her lower lip and forced a smile. "I wanted financial security."

"And you received it," he pointed out."What's the problem?"

Moriah realized their conversation wasn't moving in a positive direction."There's no problem, she said flatly, "You shall have a son." She stood and walked from the room.

The next few days Darius was edgy and the tension between them was almost palpable. What amazed Moriah was, she never would have held it against him in the past to marry for a son. This was acceptable in Malaysian society. Now she found the thought disturbing.

Moriah yearned for a real marriage. She discovered Nancy's deceit left him incapable of trust. As a result, he would distance himself from anyone who tried to get close. His intensity at times caused him to over react. Darius had no wish to be at emotional risk. Moriah was determined to help him overcome his fears to achieve the family she desperately wanted.

What was the problem? Darius wondered. Both achieved their goals. What did she expect? He was trying his best to settle into married life and share his life with a woman for chrissake. He had done well Darius patted himself on the back.

As Moriah prepared dinner for them she pondered why he had difficulty expressing himself. She wondered if he really was selfish? Or had Nancy hurt him beyond reproach?

Flustered she shook her head at the dilemma. Until Darius chose to do so, she was at loss. This was the most frustrating situation she had been involved in. Well, maybe not the most frustrating, her family's demise and her life after had been worse by far. But this situation rated high on the list.

Moriah carried the food into the dining room. She had gone to great effort to set the table attractively, and serve white wine with the fish. Given this, they dined in uncomfortable silence. After she cleared the dishes, she claimed a headache and retired for the night.

The man was impossible!

She bathed and sat down to write Kisha a letter.

He was no better at marriage than he was twenty years ago Darius realized he had made a mistake. He had no problems issuing orders but when it came to expressing himself to a woman, words failed him. He felt sorry for Moriah. Stuck with an insensitive bastard like him, how could she be anything but confused? Hell, he was.

All he wanted was a son and a ranch to pass on to his heir. If he were honest with himself, Darius wanted a woman's love much more. Everything was there for the taking. If only he could forget his anger, distrust, and his fear of being vulnerable.

He had been half crazy after finding Nancy in bed with John. At the time Darius had wanted to shoot them both. The shame she caused nearly destroyed him. Afterward he maintained an aloofness where women were concerned, seeing them only for the pleasures they could provide. For awhile this satisfied him, except one thought continued to nag him. The thought of growing old alone distressed him. It gave Darius reason to re-evaluate his life.

After she completed the letter to Kisha, Moriah considered Carrie's suggestion. First she would take a class to acquaint herself with American history. What better way to understand its people? Second she would strive to learn Western culture -- this is where Nora's instruction would help. Perhaps she'd enroll in a craft class? Nora could help Moriah to organize and manage her time effectively. Her relationship with Darius had reached a standstill. There was one thing she had learned, and learned well, he was a private man who discussed matters when he was ready and not before. He held a part of himself under wraps -- guarded like Fort Knox.

It was fortuitous Moriah thought his family's visit brought her to her senses. Their visit gave her insight into the complex man she married. And yet there were several unanswered questions. Indeed her questions wouldn't be answered at once. Moriah reached over and switched off the lamplight when the telephone rang. She lifted the receiver.

"Moriah?" Nora questioned.

"Yes?"

"I am sorry to call late but I wanted to tell you about the meeting tomorrow night."

"What meeting?"

"For the fundraiser to build a new wing for the school. You will be there?"

She wanted to focus on something besides her problems. "Yes, of course."

"Terrific. I'll pick you up at six." Nora hung up abruptly.

Moriah knew Darius expected dinner at six, but Nora hadn't allowed time for her to respond. It was only for one night, she reasoned.

~* * * *~

Monday evening arrived and Nora was knocking at the door before Moriah realized the time. She left Darius's dinner in the oven. Instead of mentioning her plans for the evening to him, she chose to leave him a note on the butcher block.

"I hope Darius won't mind," Nora began. "Sometimes the meetings last for hours."

"He'll understand."

"Good." Nora circled the drive and pulled the Ford Explorer onto the dirt road leading toward the highway.

Actually she was uncertain how he would respond to her absence. But as Carrie said, it was a time to take a stand. Fifteen minutes later Nora pulled the Explorer into the parking area of the school. They climbed out and started for the meeting. Before she knew it, eight o'clock came and went. Moriah gazed at the clock as the speaker continued past the allotted time. Much later, the speaker concluded and everyone stood. Some gathered for conversation, while others hurried to depart.

Nora deliberately kept Moriah longer than necessary. "Did you enjoy her speech?"

"Yes but she was outspoken."

"American women are liberal in their views. We stand up for what we believe in and defend women's rights to be whatever they want to become," Nora explained. "For equal pay and recognition."

"You are right," Moriah agreed.

~* * * *~

Darius was displeased to find Moriah out for the evening. He found himself dining alone once more. Darius opened the newspaper to read over dinner. He puttered around the house moving from one thing to the next, finding no satisfaction with anything. A wife belongs at home with her husband he reasoned.

Nora dropped Moriah off at nine o'clock. When she entered the house Moriah noticed Darius was asleep on the sofa. The sound must have awakened him, he began to stir.

"Have a good time?"

"Yes. But it ran much longer than I anticipated," Moriah answered. "You alright?"

He sat up indolently. "Sure."

She started for the kitchen.

"Moriah?"

She turned. "Yes?"

"Never mind." Darius rose and stretched. She cocked her head in question and stood there for a moment before continuing into the kitchen.

Tonight Darius was exhausted. He made his way into the bedroom. He almost told her he missed her not being there when he arrived home. He had given their relationship much thought.

He would strive to be more understanding. Truth was Darius had not put forth his best effort. Darius was spoiled and expected Moriah to do all the giving. Seemingly she tired of his attitude and was rebelling. He suspected Carrie had a hand in this. He admitted he had been unfair. This would change, he vowed.

On Wednesday Moriah planned to check what classes were available at Sinclair College. Again, Nora came to the rescue with transportation. During breakfast she informed Darius she would be out this afternoon. He was irritated to say the least but he accepted it.

This was the third day in a row Moriah and Nora went off together for one reason or another Darius thought. Disappointed he knew he could forget the picnic he planned earlier for them by the lake. How could they further their relationship when she wasn't home anymore? Darius considered.

"You should learn to drive, Moriah," Nora said as they walked toward the entrance of Sinclair College.

Moriah was absorbed in her own thoughts barely hearing Nora's words. "Indeed."

"They have drivers' education classes." Moriah nodded in agreement as they entered the door. The admissions office took her application and directed her to counselling. An hour later the two women drove from the school's parking lot.

"Let's go over to my place? The kids will be home soon and we can review some ideas I have for the fundraiser," Nora suggested.

"Good idea." She enjoyed Nora's company immensely. Nora included Moriah in everything and this made Moriah feel as though she belonged.

"What will Darius say when he learns what you've done?"

"I'm not sure he will approve."

"Of course not. He wants you to remain the obedient Eastern wife." Nora's affection for Moriah was reflected in her eyes.

"We'll change that." Both women chuckled as Nora gave Moriah's hand a squeeze.

Moriah was relieved to make a friend. She was lonely with Darius out on the ranch most of the time or equally distant when he was home. Determined to make the most of their friendship, Moriah vowed nothing would undermine it.

When they arrived at the Johnson home, Nora offered a diet coke which Moriah accepted readily. Moments later the children entered the kitchen. "Megan, Lisa and Tommy this is Mrs. Mc Coy. The children uttered a bashful hello. Nora's eyes were trained on Moriah as she spoke. "Megan is six, Lisa's eight, and Tommy is ten."

"Hello children," Moriah greeted each with a broad smile. She considered Nora's children polite. Minutes later they rushed out to play.

"We could have a bake sale. No. This time we should do something different. How about a potluck dinner? The monies could go toward building the new wing for the school," Nora mused.

"Better still, you're going to love this," Nora laughed. "We'll arrange a competition between Sinclair and Titus."

Moriah cast Nora a bewildered look.

"Why didn't I think of this before?" Nora supplied. "We'll have a raffle and we will ask one of the local dealerships to donate a car or truck. That should raise the money we need."

"Do you think they would be willing?"

"Don't let the small towns fool you. Both have been in competition for years. The grudge goes way back. We'll simply take advantage of this competition and see which small town can sell the most tickets and offer an additional prize. The school will reap the reward."

"Why kind of grudge?" Moriah asked.

"Who knows? It has been long ago everyone has forgotten." Both women laughed when Nora made a face. "Lamar can contact some of his friends. What about Darius, will he help?"

Moriah had no idea.

"It's no reason to look forlorn," Nora said encouraging. Moriah brightened when she made another silly face. "No problem. We'll have Lamar ask him."

Nora moved to the next matter on the agenda. "You should buy some frozen dinners, they will save valuable time. It looks as though you will be busy. Have Darius help you with the house. Lamar does the dishes and helps with the laundry. You have to break them in right." Nora waited, assessing her response. Her expression must have convinced Nora.

Moriah simply could not believe what she was hearing.

Nora shrugged. "It's true. As women we have to stick together."

The screen door opened and closed with a thud as Megan sauntered inside. "Mom, I'm hungry. Can we eat now?"

Moriah glanced at her watch, it was six o'clock. "I must go home."

Nora announced, "I have to take Mrs. Mc Coy home. Megan's pouting face brightened fractionally when Nora passed the children a snack. "C'mon, Moriah I'll take you home."

Nora did not linger after dropping Moriah off. She waved goodbye and pointed the Explorer toward the highway.

"Do you plan to forego your duties to run around with Nora?" Darius asked tersely as she entered the house.

"I know it's late, but we had so much to discuss."

"What's important that it takes all afternoon?" His face reflected disapproval.

"Today I enrolled in a history class. I plan on driving lessons as well." Moriah sat her purse on the hall table.

Darius stood in the middle of the living room, his mouth parted as if prepared to speak, then thought better of it. Apparently she surprised him, Moriah watched Darius plough a hand through his hair. He was disgusted as he muttered under his breath.

"What the hell for?"

"I want to learn to drive and everything about America." Moriah stood with her hands planted firmly on her hips, her eyes engaging his squarely.

"What's the profound interest in Nora?"

"She's gracious enough to help me. I will return her kindness by helping with the raffle." Annoyed, Moriah crossed to the armoire and poured two glasses of red wine. She held one out to him. Darius reached out for it.

"What raffle?" His expression changed to one of mild curiosity.

"The Women's Club is sponsoring a raffle to raise funds to build a new wing for the elementary school." Moriah took a large sip from her glass.

"I see."

"Do you?" She shot him a challenging look.

"I don't think my words were confusing," Darius said sarcastically. "What disturbs you?"

"You disturb me."

"I see."

"No, you don't."

"Then tell me." His voice lowered an octave. He had never seen Moriah look so determined.

"I am tired of your superior attitude as well as your lack of consideration for my feelings. You don't trust me. I feel as though I am in competition, against what I don't know." Moriah's shoulders heaved with the force of her emotions.

He moved to her side. "Don't cry," Darius coaxed softly. He couldn't bear to see her cry. Darius took her in his arms and wiped her tear-drenched cheeks with one hand. He crooked a finger and lifted her chin. Her eyes reflected confusion and pain. His head dipped.

~****~

CHAPTER 14

Darius plundered her mouth and sensibilities. His long fingers worked deftly over her shoulders and back causing her to quiver with pleasure. When she pressed her body against his Darius knew he could no longer endure the temptation. He wanted her like never before. Moriah had no trouble interpreting the silent message his eyes sent her.

"What the hell!" She heard him utter before lifting her into his arms. He pushed the bedroom door open with one foot, kicking it shut behind him. Gently he laid her on the bed and lowered himself next to her. His eyes swept over her with a tenderness Moriah had never seen. Once more his mouth covered hers. With a guttural moan Darius tore her blouse open. His hand arched over the swell of one breast, his mouth enveloped the firm rosy bud beneath. She moaned small indistinct cries of pleasure as his hand massaged and caressed her to a pinnacle of pleasure only he could provide. His skin was warm and his muscles rigid as he hovered over her, his tongue blazed a tantalizing trail. Moriah trembled convulsively. Something inside Darius clenched.

Momentarily he withdrew, ripping off his shirt. He wanted to feel her warm soft flesh against his. Moriah unfastened her jeans, pushing them to her thighs. He gave a faint grin at her efforts then helped her remove them. She wriggled her hips invitingly as she slipped out of them. It was unfair for a woman to be so utterly feminine -- to affect him in this manner. Darius unfastened his jeans and almost stumbled when one leg would not come off. He released a frustrated groan at his ineptness. He had been so intent on burying himself inside her, he almost broke his neck trying to struggle free.

Moriah was bold and if he did not take her she was convinced she may attack him!

Desire coursed in his veins, he returned to her side. Darius cupped her face in his hands and angled his mouth over hers. His kiss held all the sweet passion it had promised. She lightly ran her hand along the length of him cupping his bottom. She appreciated a tight derriere. His throbbing manhood on her thigh sent its own pulsing message through her. Every nerve and cell in her body danced a primal rhythm. He arched his back and entered her soft moistness with a determined thrust of his hips. Darius lifted her hips for deeper penetration. He groaned with the sheer pleasure of it.

"Moriah, you drive me crazy with wanting you."

His confession stunned Moriah. She delighted in knowing she had the power to shatter his defenses. A spasm began to work its way outward from her core. Her body tingled all over as a liquid warmness washed over her. She had no idea pleasure like this existed. He was masterful in the art of lovemaking.

Until now Moriah wondered if anyone could penetrate his shield. All her suppressed emotions surfaced, a desire for a real marriage with respect, trust and a willingness to communicate freely.

"I do?"

"Yes. I'm like a man whose been isolated ... " Darius's voice trailed off. The sweet excitement claimed his sensibilities and Darius gave into it.

Instinctively Moriah moved to the rhythm, delighting in the feel and taste of him. "I love you, Darius."

He just increased the tempo of their lovemaking, presently he paused during her words.

Moriah had not meant for the words to escape, however she was one who spoke honestly -- and this definitely was heaven on earth. "Don't stop," she urged in a throaty voice. Slowly he began to rock his hips. "Yes!"

Darius had never experienced a sense of belonging. Lately it seemed he couldn't get his fill of her. Possessing this woman was second only to breathing. He hated to admit she occupied his thoughts most of the time. Darius knew he could not bear to be without Moriah. The mere thought distressed him. His body trembled convulsively as his seed poured into her. Darius collapsed against her and Moriah clutched him tightly.

Much later she lay nestled in his arms, staring at the ceiling. The steady rise and fall of his chest indicated he had fallen asleep. The impact of her feelings for him struck her all at once. She had never felt so strongly. This chauvinistic male bewildered her. She cherished tenderness, honesty and respect in a relationship. Darius sorely tested everything she held dear.

This would not be easy in any event their relationship had taken a new meaning. She could not define the change but they had grown closer. At least Darius welcomed her into his life and trusted her. She would not betray his trust. At long last Moriah drifted to sleep her body intertwined with his.

The next few days passed happily. Moriah had a week to indulge her husband before classes started. She began to see subtle changes in Darius. Today he planned a picnic for them by the lake. He claimed he had a surprise for her. The noon sun shined brightly overhead as Darius stopped the Land Cruiser alongside the gazebo. He uncoiled his six-foot-five frame from behind the wheel and helped her climb out.

"How marvelous," Moriah exclaimed. The gazebo could easily accommodate eight to ten people. She could see the pride in his eyes as he spoke.

"I'm glad you approve." Amusement glinted in his eyes as he held her swimsuit just out of her reach. "Let's go for a dip before lunch," Darius suggested with a mischievous grin.

Moriah shifted her gaze to the lake. The heat from the sun was fierce and the lake was more than inviting she thought. Her face brightened with enthusiasm. Looking to each side for onlookers, Moriah snatched her swimsuit from him.

"You little prude." He laughed a throaty baritone sound that pleased her. Moriah scrambled out of her clothes. Once she slipped into her suit, she ran into the water.

"It pleased him to see her happy and smiling. He never wanted to see her cry again. Darius realized with a start he wanted to protect her. Her undaunted freshness of spirit and sensitivity enthralled him. Watching her made his loins ache with desire, his sensibilities sharpen. The evidence of his errant thoughts embarrassed him. Darius turned his back to Moriah and stepped into his suit.

Darius remembered what an army buddy's once told him, "When I was younger, I used to be a terror in bed. Now, I'm more like a terrier." He chuckled to himself. Indeed this was not the case with him. If anything the urge grew stronger each day. He dove into the cool water. He must be mad he considered, they should be skinny-dipping. He felt a familiar tightness in his loins. He hoped the cool water would help but he remained hard almost to the point of pain.

She surfaced the water shaking her head when he moved toward her. The seductive gleam in his eyes startled her. Oh no, he wouldn't? His mouth covered hers in a heartbeat. She could feel each curve of his male form.

Feverishly he pushed the straps from her shoulders, his lips and tongue savoring her rosy buds. They removed their garments as Darius dove under the water. Before she realized what was happening he managed to anchor their bodies against the gazebo's forms that dropped into the lake below. He slid upward along her length with deliberate strokes, grasping her waist he lifted her slightly. Moriah wrapped her legs around his waist as he thrust his hips upward, penetrating her feminine core.

The undulating sensations were almost more than Moriah could bear. What sweet heaven! She considered herself fortunate to have a man of infinite passion. Darius made her blood rush and her body cry that he should never stop. His lips and hands caressed her, urging her to respond. The ecstasy was almost Moriah's undoing. Her body trembled under his tender touch. She fell victim to the sensations.

They returned to shore some time later. After slipping into their swimsuits they began to lay out the picnic supplies. Why had she readily accepted him? Why the sudden attack of conscious? Moriah considered earlier he had neglected her shamelessly. Now he longed for her. Was he trustworthy? Moriah wondered. A man who didn't not know how to treat a woman. Moriah took a deep breath, releasing her tension. She must relax she told herself and forget her doubts.

With an expression of male satisfaction, Darius commented, "This is my idea of a picnic." He bit into the chicken breast with fervor.

Suddenly the hair at her nape stood on end. Moriah remembered his motivation for marrying her -- to have a son! She forced a smile and tried to push the thought to the back of her mind. They made polite conversation but the dreaded thought continued to disturb Moriah.

He disturbed her silent reverie. "We had better get back."

Moriah was stunned. "Just like that?" she asked incredulously. "How can you be so mechanical is beyond me?"

Her insinuation and the tone of her voice grated on Darius. "Earlier you weren't exactly fighting me off, lady." Darius drew the last word out for effect. The inflection of his voice indicated she was anything but. He turned and gathered the supplies.

The comment was unfair and he knew it, Moriah thought. For this reason it hurt all the more. She considered that history has a way of repeating itself. They rode back to the house in pregnant silence. Each time she thought the relationship progressed, they took two steps back. Moriah discovered she developed a temper of her own. She had caused the disagreement between them at the lake, however she justified her actions with her intense longing to prolong their happiness for as long as possible. Her outburst back at the lake had even surprised Moriah. She admitted silently she behaved childishly.

Darius launched himself out of the Land Cruiser as soon as he turned off the ignition. Moriah closed the door he carelessly left open. Darius was so angry he was speechless. The woman confused him to no end. Hell, yeah, he wanted a son. What of it? What did she expect anyway? He was honest about his intentions from the beginning. What made her so unpredictable? She had no cause to attack him that way! Women were fickle he considered. Moriah had done him a favor to remind him of this. Up to a point they were getting along until now. He expected the relationship to take a turn for the worse. What a woman would not do at times was criminal, Darius thought. If she wanted it this way, he would oblige her. Besides he relished his own time.

Moriah started classes on Monday evening.

Darius disliked being alone while Moriah ran around with Nora. Maybe he was jealous of Nora he considered? Darius didn't believe this, but he confessed he would be pleased when she returned home.

When Moriah returned at ten that evening, she discovered him asleep on the sofa with the stereo playing soft jazz. She smiled and covered him with an afghan and turned the stereo off.

The next day began as any other day by preparing her husband's breakfast. Moriah telephoned Nora after seeing him off for the day.

"Am I glad you called," Nora greeted. "Listen the girls think the raffle's a great idea. The tickets will be ready this afternoon.

"We have you to thank."

Nora dismissed the compliment. "How many would you like Moriah?"

"I'll start with twenty."

"How is Darius taking your absence?"

"Actually he has been sweet. He has changed since his family's visit" Moriah said with bravado, hearing the disbelief in her voice.

"How do you mean?" Nora prodded.

"Darius seems," Moriah searched for the right word then continued, "more human. Vulnerable. Yes, vulnerable."

"That's called progress," Nora replied. "Let's get together this afternoon?"

"I would love to, but I cannot," Moriah confessed. There was a long silence, then she continued, "I have a doctor's appointment."

"What's wrong?"

"I have been nauseated and -"

"That's wonderful," Nora interrupted. "You're going to have a baby!"

"I hope that's all. I feel terrible." Moriah seemingly brought Nora's motherly instincts to the forefront.

"When's your appointment?"

"Two o'clock."

"Your doctor in Austin?"

"Yes. Why?"

"I'll pick you up at twelve forty-five." Moments later Nora rang off.

Moriah decided to start the housework if she planned to be ready on time. She purposely chose today for the doctor's visit. Darius would be away most of the day. He and Jason left early this morning for a small town north of Austin to purchase a young bull for breeding purposes.

Nora arrived on schedule and they proceeded to Austin.

Later that afternoon at Nora's house, Moriah leaned back on the over-stuffed chair. "I had a feeling, I was pregnant. But I still cannot believe it."

"Think how happy Darius will be when he finds out," Nora commented, sipping her lemonade.

Moriah was concerned. Soon Darius would realize the son he desperately wanted. Their marriage would return to what Darius intended originally -- a matter of convenience. Inside she was sick and it had nothing to do with the baby. Moriah had hoped he would grow to love her.

"You don't seem happy about it," Nora pointed out.

"It's not that," Moriah explained. "Darius wants a child, a son."

"And you don't?" Nora asked incredulously. Shrugging, she forged ahead. "I sense a celebration in store."

Moriah's voice was distracted. "Huh?"

Nora repeated the statement. "What's wrong?"

"I'm not going to tell him."

Nora laughed sarcastically. "Why?"

"You have to trust me on this one," Moriah replied. "Promise me you won't mention a word of this to anyone?"

Nora shot her a puzzled look.

"Promise me?"

"I don't understand the secrecy," Nora shrugged and threw her hands up. "But, I promise."

"Give me the raffle tickets," Moriah said anxiously. "I must go."

"Okay little mother, I will take you home."

On the way over to the Mc Coy ranch, Moriah spoke, "We'll keep our sessions on Monday, Wednesdays and Fridays after my classes. She slanted her eyes at Nora, waiting for an answer.

Nora thought Moriah was being evasive. "Why won't you tell me?"

"I have to work things out for myself," Moriah answered with a grin. "I will explain later. I promise."

It was four o'clock when Nora and Moriah arrived at the Mc Coy ranch. Moriah hurried inside and changed into jeans and a blouse, after throwing herself on the bed. Darius has his wish at last, Moriah thought only she had no intention of telling him.

~* * * *~

CHAPTER 15

The first light of dawn reared its head, yet Moriah hadn't slept a wink. She sat on the bedside several moments considering her predicament. Why couldn't she bring herself to tell him? Moriah thought. He desires this a great deal? She was not a vengeful person. Then why? Moriah was afraid he would resort to treating her like a stranger, instead of his wife. They had become close. No she wouldn't risk the progress they had made by telling him. At least until she had time to consider the situation in a calm and collected manner.

During breakfast, Darius lifted his head from the paper. "How are your classes coming?"

He sounded genuinely interested. This touched Moriah's heart. She need more time. Time to explore his true feelings and where she fit into his life.

"Very well." She smiled, "I am a quick study."

"Marvelous." Darius could not believe his words. "When will you help with the raffle?"

"I have some tickets to sell, now."

Reaching inside his pocket, Darius said, "I'll take four." His smile was reflected in his eyes as Darius peered over the newspaper at her.

Moriah smiled. "How wonderful."

"I thought we might get away for awhile," Darius explained. When she remained silent, he continued, "We never had a honeymoon. We could take a couple of weeks and see the country," he suggested.

"What a lovely thought."

"I mean it, Moriah. Jason can handle things while we're away. Two weeks in a log cabin on a lake in the Ozarks. How does this sound?" Darius prodded softly.

"I'd really like to, but ..."

His smile changed to a frown. "But what?"

She lowered her eyes. "I cannot."

"I thought you would be pleased," Darius commented blandly, his anger building. He bit his tongue.

"You've made me happy just by asking," Moriah confessed. "I have classes. Perhaps, later?"

Who could figure women! Darius thought. He disliked the word, no. "I don't understand, Moriah. What's more important? Your silly classes? Or us?" Darius ground out.

"Silly? You think, they're silly?" Her voice was short and clipped, now. Her brown eyes flashing fire, her face flushed with emotion, Moriah stood and crossed to the stove. She made jerky movements to clear the counter.

The pitch of her voice made her sound like the mad hatter he chuckled silently. "Of course they're silly," Darius remarked weary of her theatrics. "Simply withdraw. You can sign up anytime."

Her hands were planted firmly on her hips as she turned to face him. "I won't do it!" Moriah snapped.

"That's the damndest thing I have ever heard." His laughter held a sneering quality.

"I'm sorry you feel this way," she hissed. "Nothing is worthy of your attention, unless it's your idea."

"Forget I mentioned it. It wasn't important." He rose and threw his napkin on the table, crossing the room in seconds.

Surely he wasn't leaving? Moriah thought.

Darius never altered his stride as he continued out the door. The back door resounded with a slam behind him.

Moriah was incensed.

He could stomp out the door forever like a spoiled child she thought. He was asking her to choose between her self-esteem and what he wanted. This was a *power play* Moriah considered. Nora had warned her of this. If she allowed him to run roughshod over her now, there would be no end to it. Moriah was one to adapt easily to Western culture, she would not easily submit. There was more at stake here Moriah thought, than a trip -- their whole relationship! Or lack of one? She would find out. Colonel Mc Coy has met his Waterloo she considered.

~* * * *~

Darius drove out to look at the new bull he purchased yesterday. They had done well, the bull was a bargain just as Jason said. The herd would increase with the breeding he planned to do. Too bad it wasn't that simple with women. Why they made life complicated was beyond him. No matter how hard he tried, Darius was not adept at marriage. Most women would gladly accept the romantic interlude he suggested, except Moriah. Darius had taken Ben's suggestion to romance her seriously. He never considered she might refuse. He had simply taken for granted she would go along.

Maybe her life in Malaysia had been difficult, she was unable to recognize a good thing? Why did she care more for her classes than being with him? Maybe he possessed a trait that women just did not respond to well? She claimed to love him, in any event what was the problem? Either she reconsidered her decision or he simply would leave without her. The time apart might help set her priorities straight Darius thought. He wanted to seriously consider the relationship. Two weeks should provide him ample time.

Moriah hadn't labored over lunch otherwise she might have been annoyed when Darius didn't come home for lunch. The man had a few lessons to learn about women. Perhaps time spent alone would help Darius see matters in perspective Moriah reasoned.

That afternoon Nora dropped by early for Moriah. They planned to sell raffle tickets at the school car wash. "Lamar will meet us," Nora explained as Moriah stepped into the Explorer. When she remained silent, Nora questioned, "What's wrong?"

"He is stubborn at times," Moriah blurted.

"This has the ear marks of a fight." Nora rallied to the cause.

"Whenever I consider something important, Darius thinks it's trivial. What he wants is all that matters."

"He does come across as demanding at times. Did you tell him about the baby?"

"This is exactly the reason, I cannot tell him."

"I give. Tell me."

"It is simple. He is lord and master. Whatever he wants, he expects. I'm merely a pawn to achieve his goal."

"Pray tell, what is this?"

"He wants a son to carry on his precious name." Moriah's voice dripped with sarcasm.

"You want to be appreciated for yourself, not because of the baby." Nora realized with a start. "You poor thing. How awful for you."

Moriah's demeanor softened slightly. "He can be gentle and concerned one moment, and demanding and obstinate the next."

"I thought older men were more settled." Nora shook her head in disbelief. "What if I ask Lamar to speak to him?"

"I'll handle this my way." Forcing a smile she pointed into the crowd and said, "Look there's a good turn out this afternoon for the car wash. We'll sell a lot of tickets."

"That's the spirit."

~* * * *~

Darius arrived at two o'clock to find the house empty. Her absence solidified his decision. He lifted the telephone receiver and punched out the numbers. He waited for a connection. "The name is Mc Coy. I would like to book a cabin for two weeks." He paused to listen. "That will be fine. I prefer one starting tomorrow. Thank you." He broke the connection.

Darius moved in the direction of the bedroom to pack. Moriah could decide her priorities he thought as he threw his clothes into a suitcase. If he was not important enough to her, perhaps he had best cut his losses and both part ways?

Was Moriah worth fighting for? Where did that come from? Darius wondered. He dismissed the thought immediately. Caught in his reverie, he almost forgot to book a flight. He lifted the receiver once more.

~* * * *~

With Lamar's help, Nora and Moriah sold all the raffle tickets they had taken along. The neighboring towns Sinclair and Titus planned similar fund raising events this afternoon Moriah learned. She became enthralled with the competition and soon forgot her problems.

"Lamar managed to have the Chevrolet dealership in Sinclair to donate a truck," Nora beamed. "He said -"

"Folks can always use a truck," Lamar interrupted.

"How did you ever do it?" Moriah asked approvingly.

"Just used my charm," Lamar boasted.

Afterward Moriah was off to her driving class while Nora started for her meeting.

After class and a short session with Nora, Moriah was pleased to return home. Why was the house dark she wondered? Once inside Moriah called in a small voice, "Darius?" When no response was forthcoming, she went through the house flipping the lights on. She discovered a note on the dining table that read:

Moriah, I've gone to Arkansas for two weeks. I need to get away for awhile. If you care to join me, here's where I'll be. Darius

At the bottom of Darius's note was the address and telephone number along with directions to his whereabouts. If she cares to join him? What gall the man has! Moriah paced the floor calling him arrogant, stubborn, demanding, petty, spoiled and anything else she could think of. The man was insufferable!

After the tirade she resolved to hold firmly to her decision. Let him mull things over. If he wanted to disregard her wishes they had nothing on which to base a relationship. Moriah cried herself to sleep that night.

She fought to stay awake Thursday morning. The nausea claimed her energy most days. What a combination Moriah mused, morning sickness -- a physical ailment; but what does one do for a broken heart? Her reflection in the mirror fit her mood. Her skin was pasty and her hair dull and dry. Moriah brooded wondering what madness overcame her to marry a self-serving male.

After lunch Nora telephoned about the carnival in Sinclair. Even Nora's enthusiasm failed to lift Moriah's spirits. Purposefully she tried to inject the right amount of enthusiasm into her voice -- which she most assuredly did not feel. If Nora noticed, she did not mention it.

Two days passed without a word from Moriah, Darius thought as he sat by the lake in the Ozarks. Even the fish were not biting. His anger subsided, though replaced by skepticism. Maybe there was nothing to salvage? This was the reason Moriah hadn't contacted him. She was relieved he made the decision for her.

He tried to enjoy fishing, hiking and he had even tried one of the massage houses in Hot Springs but his restlessness continued unabated. He wasn't sure what he wanted anymore. He felt empty inside, without purpose. Darius kept asking himself the same question over and over -- why?

On the eve of the fourth day, Darius could bear this no longer. The solitude was driving him mad. He had to speak to someone. He telephoned Julie Cunningham.

"You're the last person I expected to call," Julie greeted. "What a surprise, Darius."

"I shouldn't have called," Darius responded. When she remained silent, he continued, "I'm sorry."

"Look Darius, we go back a long way," Julie explained. Her tone seemed to soothe him. "You can call me anytime."

"I know this may sound ludicrous but do you find me overbearing at times?" Darius asked.

"Well, just a tad. Why?"

He continued, "Self-centered? Cynical, perhaps?"

"What is this?" The joking inflection left her voice.

"Please, Julie. Answer my question."

"Why is my opinion suddenly important to you?

"Julie."

"Is this some kind of joke?" Julie responded. "Have you been drinking, Darius?" When he pushed for an answer, she replied, "Yes. You're all those things. Satisfied?"

Her pouting tone disturbed Darius but he pressed on. "Then what attracted you to me?"

"I've had enough of this!" Julie cried.

Darius lowered his voice to a tone he found worked better with women. He repeated the question.

"It happens, I prefer strong male types. I like a man who takes charge." Julie paused. "Do you plan to return to North Carolina?"

"Maybe."

"What's this about?"

"I have some personal business to attend," Darius hedged.

"Darius, I don't find this amusing."

He remained silent for a moment. "Thanks for being honest, Julie. You have been a great help. I'll be in touch." He hung up.

Julie seemed genuinely surprised by his straight forwardness and his vulnerability. This surprised Darius too. He reasoned in the past he struck others as an arrogant son-of-a-gun. He'd built a wall around himself. His fear of rejection was reason enough. Had he carried this too far?

~* * * *~

 **CHAPTER 16**

Back at the Mc Coy ranch Moriah prepared to take her driver's test. She was competent after two weeks of instruction. Darius had been away in the Ozarks for a week. She would not let this disturb her, she had a driving test to take. Moriah wanted to be independent. Nora drove her to the Department of Public Safety in Sinclair and they went inside.

Apprehension filled Moriah as she waited for the results. Finally a little man announced she had passed the written part. She was instructed to go outside and wait in her car. An officer would join her momentarily. She nodded then turned to look over her shoulder at Nora before moving to her car.

Moriah smiled as she climbed behind the wheel of the Cadillac Eldorado. She had taken the liberty of employing Darius's prized possession for her driving test. She thought dismally he prized everything over her. Presently the police officer approached the passenger side of the car appraising it as he moved. Perhaps she'd made a mistake? Why was he so smug in appearance? Or was it her imagination? It's nerves she told herself. Relax!

The officer gave Moriah brief instructions. She started the car and pulled into traffic. The driving portion of the exam seemed to take hours, even days. At last he instructed her to turn around and return to the station. She complied.

Moriah stopped the engine as instructed. He continued to write on a clipboard he carried. Why did he look as if someone just died in his family? She goofed back there -- parallel parking and the light at the intersection turned red as she drove through it. Could she do anything right?

Finally he lifted his head and turned to her. "Congratulations, ma'am. You passed. We will chalk the errors to nervousness. "He did not wait for her response. "Fine looking machine, I've always wanted one." He shook his head appreciatively as he turned to walk away.

Moriah brought her palms to cup her face, her elbows rested on the steering wheel, a sound of relief escaped her, "Whew!" It was a small victory, but a victory nevertheless she thought. Now she could travel at will. Nora would be pleased.

Both women agreed to celebrate over dessert. "I feel frivolous," Moriah beamed. "How about a hot fudge sundae?" The waitress took the order and returned within minutes with their treat.

Nora responded with a chuckle, lifting her glass. "Here's to your independence. You have earned it."

Moriah heard the pride in Nora's voice.

"Here's to the Americanization of Moriah," Nora boasted. "My work is done."

Moriah smiled as she lifted her glass in salute. Who ever heard of a hot fudge sundae toast? she thought? Nora had this effect on her, at times, she had the silliest thoughts.

"And here's to good friends, like you. You've helped me realize my potential," Moriah added. "This is something I shall never forget."

Nora blushed. "The carnival is tonight. Can you make it by six?"

"No problem. It will be my pleasure." They embraced one another and lingered a few minutes over conversation then left the restaurant.

Later that evening Moriah drove to the carnival. Her gaze swept the large group but Nora was nowhere to be found. Seated behind the booth, Moriah began her spiel to sell raffle tickets to those passing by. The crowd buzzed with conversation and laughter and the occasional sound of a wailing child could be heard. An hour later there was still, no sign of Nora. The raffle tickets dwindled on the table. It was unusual for Nora not to show. An emergency would be the only reason for her absence Moriah thought.

Alas, a teary-faced Nora appeared in the distance. Anxiously Moriah hurried over to find a replacement for the booth, then moved purposefully toward Nora.

Moriah gathered Nora and led her away from the crowd. After taking a seat on a nearby bench, Moriah questioned, "What is wrong?"

"One of my kids, my little one Megan had an accident," Nora began, sniffling.

Moriah shot Nora an alarmed look. "What happened?"

"The kids were playing and one of them pushed Megan down and she cut her hand."

"Is she alright?"

"I don't know for sure."

"What do you mean?"

"I took the kids to stay with my parents for a couple of weeks," Nora supplied. "They called from the emergency room to tell us about it."

"What exactly did they say?"

"Lamar took the call," Nora commented. Presently her cellular phone rang. "Hold on, I need to take this. "Hello? Yes. Ok. I see. How bad was it? What does the doctor say? Oh, okay. Fine. Thanks for calling." Nora turned back to Moriah, relief apparent in her expression.

"Is everything alright?" Moriah questioned.

"Lamar is on his way to my parents to check on them. And yes, he said Megan is fine. The cut was deep, but she's fine. She fell back and cut her hand on a piece of glass on the ground. It took fifteen stitches to close the cut between her thumb and index finger of the right hand." Nora was visibly shaken.

"Since Lamar will be out of town, why don't you come over to my place? You should not be alone tonight," Moriah suggested. It was wonderful to be needed she thought. Nora nodded in agreement. Moriah led the way to the parking area. "Where is your Explorer?"

"It wouldn't start. Lamar dropped me off. I was hoping you could give me a ride home? He drove the truck to my parents."

"No problem. We will take a little detour." Moriah smiled affectionately. Nora always came through for her, Moriah planned to return the friendship and good will.

She drove to the Mc Coy ranch and parked the Cadillac Eldorado convertible. Once seated in their living room, Moriah listened attentively to Nora describe the emergency.

"That settles it," Moriah added, "What we need is a glass of wine. The world will look better afterward."

"It couldn't hurt." Nora's voice reflected her concern. "Will Darius mind in if I stay overnight?"

"Uh, no." She stood with her back to Nora, avoiding eye contact.

"I hear the hesitancy in your voice," Nora said. "Did I come at a bad time?"

"Darius is not here." For an extended moment, they were silent. She knew Nora was waiting for an answer. Moriah poured two glasses of merlot, passing one to her friend. Nora reached out, accepting the glass. "He asked me to go away with him," she confessed. "When I refused, he left without me." There she said it. Moriah placed her glass to her lips, taking a large sip.

"Are the two of you getting along?" Nora asked in amazement.

"No, we're not," Moriah responded. "He's stubborn and demanding."

"I thought you were happy?" Nora drank half the glass of wine.

"When he gets his way everything's fine," Moriah explained in a low tone. "For awhile, I thought he would change. After years of living alone, who knows?" Moriah's voice trailed off.

"You sound as though, you're giving up."

"I have considered the matter for some time. I'm leaving Darius. Some men should never marry – he's one of them."

"When you tell him about the baby, he won't allow you to leave."

"I'm leaving for Austin before he returns."

"What about work?"

"I speak four languages. Perhaps I can be an interpreter."

Nora moved toward Moriah. "I will miss you." The women embraced.

"Promise me, you will not tell him where I've gone?"

"If that's what you want?"

Moriah's eyes narrowed. "He wants the baby, not me. The problem is I could never give up my baby, just hand it over to him. I will leave and take the baby with me."

"He has a right to know about the child," Nora reminded.

"After I have settled, I will tell Darius. I want him to gradually grow accustomed to the idea."

"Do you love him?"

"Yes. But love is not enough. For a relationship to survive, there must be respect, trust, and a willingness to give -- to allow the person you love to be himself or herself."

"That's beautiful," Nora blubbered. "I hope I haven't caused problems between the two of you?"

"I'm not the same woman he married. But no, we're splitting because of his domineering ways and his distrust."

Nora shot her a fretful look.

"It would have happened eventually. You helped me see things more clearly." She turned and leaned to embrace Nora, patting her affectionately on the back. "I will always cherish our friendship."

Nora began to cry. "But you don't have a family or friends here, except us. I'll worry about you."

"I appreciate your concern," Moriah said softly. She crossed her arms at the waist. "And I have someone dependent on me. I will stay in touch." She lifted her proud chin. "Don't worry, we will be fine."

"You are one in a million, Moriah."

The grandfather clock in the hallway announced the tenth hour and they retired for the night.

~* * * *~

Carrie kept playing the scene over in her head. Since she returned to Arizona, she couldn't think of anything but Ben Willis. She chalked her recent madness up to celibacy. Finally it had taken its toll. She was reduced to mooning over a kiss, how pathetic Carrie thought.

She remembered that night with Ben at the dance. The unforgettable night in Sinclair, Texas. Never had Carrie felt so alive. She would never forget the kiss. It was tender and promised great passion. When their lips met for the first time, Carrie felt as though a bolt of lightning travelled through her.

"You're the most beautiful woman here tonight," Ben whispered in Carrie's ear as they slow danced.

Carrie was convinced Ben could conquer the world. He was dashing and witty. She never grew weary of his company. Ordinarily she wouldn't be taken back by a man with red hair, but Ben was special. He was a liberated male, secure in himself. Carrie knew she intimidated most men with her intelligence. She tired of the pretense, if they were insecure that was their problem. Ben appreciated her spirit and intelligence.

Ben's intelligence wasn't what attracted Carrie most, but his free spirit and attitude about life. He dared to be himself and she found this refreshing in a man. She wanted a man who would make her feel desirable as a woman. A man who could love her and Chris, someone who she could share her aspirations of working for herself in research. Carrie realized Ben was part hype; regardless, she liked his style. Inside she felt warm and beautiful. Everyone wanted and needed to feel appreciated Carrie reasoned, it was good to feel alive.

Carrie had to forget the nonsense she thought later that same night. Carrie laughed at herself she was beginning to sound like a dime novel. Fantasies are entertaining but life is another matter. Chris was her life she had to focus. Besides, she probably would never see Ben Willis again.

~* * * *~

Moriah leaned back against the sofa and opened the classified section of the Austin paper. She had to locate a new home and a job. It was times like this, she was grateful Darius placed their bank accounts in both names.

By Tuesday Moriah was settled in her new townhouse in Austin. A stack of boxes served as a make shift chair until the furniture arrived. Moriah gazed around the empty townhouse and few boxes that cluttered the living room. Now, she was on her own. Moriah knew she made the transition at the perfect time, while Darius was away. He was scheduled to return tomorrow. She took a taxi to Austin -- which left her on foot. Oh well, there was the bus system. Moriah considered the townhouse small, just the same if she arranged it right this could work to meet her needs. She would turn the extra bedroom into a nursery. She rubbed her stomach and smiled, at two and half months her size remained unchanged.

She would look for a job in a few days. Tonight Moriah planned to relax. Luckily her clothes and toiletries were the only items she brought with her from Sinclair. Yesterday she purchased living and bedroom furniture. It was scheduled for delivery today. Moriah hoped at least the bed arrived. The empty townhouse could use the furniture. Still she needed several items and additional furniture but she would slowly acquire them.

This was a new adventure she embarked upon Moriah told herself. She lifted her plastic glass in silent salute to her new life. Their new life together -- hers and the baby's, Moriah corrected silently.

~* * * *~

Darius returned a day earlier than expected because he was anxious to see Moriah. He discovered the house in complete darkness. This was strange he thought. What was happening? He found a note in the kitchen and read:

Darius, I see no hope for our relationship, so I've moved out. We're two strangers who should never have met. I do not blame you totally nor do I hold a grudge. I wish you every happiness. Please do not look for me. It's better this way. Moriah

He blinked in disbelief. He disliked the feeling he experienced in his stomach as he read the note. Darius strode into the dining room and poured a glass of brandy and downed it -- pouring another. With the glass in hand, he slumped into a chair. The thought never occurred to him she might leave. He felt as though his heart had suddenly been ripped from his chest. He took a large swallow of brandy from the glass.

As usual, he discovered his ignorance too late. Darius thought this was the only word that described his behavior. Where was she? He missed Moriah terribly and he'd returned a day earlier than expected just to be with her. Over the past two weeks it had taken all his self restraint to keep from telephoning her. Darius yearned for her soft voice and smile. He ventured to say he sounded as though he was in love. Love? No! He was incapable of this emotion.

He read the note again. It sounds so final! There must be a way? For what a small voice within him queried. To tell her, I love her!

Where would he begin to search for her? Who would know where she was? Nora. That's it! He grabbed the telephone and punched out the number. There was no answer. He cradled the phone. This served him right she had left. He did not blame her. Darius considered himself a fool. After several unsuccessful attempts to reach Nora, he tied one on that night.

~* * * *~

**CHAPTER 17**

Moriah did not sleep well the first night in her new home. Bleary-eyed, she decided to look for work on Thursday. She spent Wednesday unpacking boxes and arranging the townhouse. A trip to the corner grocery store solved her immediate needs.

Her evening meal in hand, Moriah sat on the sofa, employing the remote control she turned on the television. Tonight on channel eleven was *The Comancheros*, a John Wayne film. Moriah loved John Wayne, she settled back on the cushions to watch.

This morning Darius woke with a terrible hangover. He traipsed into the kitchen after a shower. His pounding head felt the size of a basketball. The fog slowly lifted from his head after three cups of coffee. He tried to call Nora to no avail. Where had everyone gone? He glanced at the clock on the kitchen wall -- ten-thirty. The place was unusually quiet for a Wednesday, ordinarily he could hear Jason puttering around in the yard or the dogs barking. And, what was worse yet -- Moriah was gone! Given the circumstances he was amazed she hadn't left sooner. Ben and Carrie tried to warn him. Even his parents in their own subtle way had offered to help, but he was stubborn and disregarded everyone's advice.

Darius cursed.

Since retirement his decision making capabilities had deteriorated. Maybe it was senility? No. Stupidity. He alone had caused his life to be disrupted. Out of desperation, his wife left him. The rejection was almost more than he could bear. Here he was a forty-four year old man, alone. Subconsciously he set out to drive her away Darius decided, and he accomplished this. His fears were his nemesis. His fear of rejection, fear if he gave to much of himself. He hadn't required enemies to realize his projected unhappiness. His fears and mistrust had pushed her away. Darius was convinced he had reached his all time low.

What would he do?

Think rationally Darius told himself. If he could reach Nora, she would know where to find Moriah. Due to the circumstances, the separation and his hangover he was inclined to take the day for rest and relaxation. Perhaps he could find his center and focus. When he was unsuccessful Thursday and Friday trying to reach Nora, Darius considered she'd left the country. Was this a conspiracy? Darius had only himself to blame.

With each day he realized more a fit of temper. Even the dogs would turn tail and run when he approached. Jason had been supportive however he'd been no help as to Moriah's whereabouts. For three days the phone was silent. As if the world said, "Okay, you want to be alone? We shall leave you alone."

Darius discovered he was not the loner he thought he was. He'd acclimated to his life with Moriah much quicker than he ever imagined. He longed for her with a fierceness. He discovered he loved her more than he thought himself capable. Considering her absence, he felt a terrible emptiness without her.

Saturday he was more restless as ever. He opted for a trip into Austin -- to ask some questions. Maybe someone knew of her whereabouts? If nothing else, he would get out of the house -- the walls were beginning to close in.

A trip to the places they frequented left him without a clue. It was as though she had vanished. Weary of the fruitless search, he treated himself to lunch. Later that afternoon he went shopping then started back at five for the ranch. Darius unloaded the Land Cruiser of his purchases and threw a frozen dinner into the microwave. Settling before the television with a rented video, he took a swallow of his iced tea. Unable to focus on the movie, he lifted the receiver and punched out a number. Darius started to hang up when Nora answered the phone.

"Thank goodness you're there."

"Darius?"

"Yes." He heaved a deep sigh.

Nora dreaded his inevitable question. Would she break her promise to Moriah? His voice reflected pain she had experienced personally. But she had given her word, Nora reminded herself. The man has a right to know about his child! He deserved a chance to reconcile their differences. His voice reflected a humility Nora hadn't heard. Only love could bring this kind of pain and humility to the spirit she surmised. Nora weighed her options.

"Where is she?" His voice was a little more than a whisper.

He hadn't wasted time with pleasantries Nora thought he came straight to the point. Silence followed.

"Nora don't play games with me. Where's my wife?"

Moriah would murder her but she couldn't bear to hear the tormented voice on the other end. "Austin."

His heart lightened. "Where exactly?"

Nora rattled off the address and telephone number. "I hope Moriah will forgive me."

"Thanks, Nora. You won't be sorry." Darius rang off.

Nora dialed Carrie's number.

Darius started to telephone Moriah but thought better of it.

Moriah was reading a romance novel when she heard a knock at the door. Who would call at this hour? She glanced at the clock on her bedside table, eight-thirty. Fear welled inside she didn't know anyone in Austin.

Whomever it was, they were persistent. Again she heard the rapping sound. She'd forgotten to secure a means of protection against intruders. A woman living alone was surely a target for crime. After slipping into her robe, she moved slowly toward the door.

"Who is it?" Moriah called through the door.

"Moriah, open the door."

How did he find her? Nora! A tiny voice within her supplied. Reluctantly she swung the door open and stepped aside to allow him entry.

A haggard man with circles under his eyes came into view. Moriah could not believe her eyes as Darius stepped inside the door. "How are you?" she began, concern lacing her voice. "Please have a seat."

"This isn't a social call."

"Why are you here?" she asked with bravado.

"To take you home where you belong."

"Just like that?" Moriah said tartly.

"Yes."

"You haven't learned a thing about me," she accused. "Did you ask if I wanted to come home? No. Did you ask why I left? No." Moriah rattled the questions and answers in rapid succession.

"No, I didn't," he conceded.

"It's like you to run roughshod over me. Also to do my thinking for me," she began. "In case you haven't noticed, I'm an intelligent, beautiful woman." Her anger building with each word.

"I know."

Seemingly he was unaffected by her outburst. Flustered, she continued, "Look around, I live here now. So you can just go away."

"When I've had my say." The deadly tone of his voice claimed her attention. It was madness for her to think he would surrender so easily.

Resigned to listening to what he had to say, Moriah asked, "Would you like a cup of hot chocolate?" Darius nodded graciously. She moved into the kitchen.

Darius released the breath he had been holding as he lowered himself onto the sofa.

She returned minutes later with two steaming cups and set them on the coffee table. When he remained silent, Moriah prodded, "What was it you wanted to say?"

"We've had to overcome our differences -- not merely as strangers, but cultural differences as well."   He paused. "I should have been a better husband to you. I've been a damn fool."

"And that should resolve everything?" Moriah managed.

He forced back an angry retort. "We can reconcile our differences only by staying together. I've had time to weigh things and ..." Glancing at his feet, Darius's voice trailed off.

Moriah was sure she'd missed some of the conversation along the way. Did he really expect her to succumb so mindlessly? Her eyes searched his. Was it disappointment she saw in his eyes? Anxiety? Frustration? Or loneliness?

"Darius, do you honestly think for one moment you could change?"

"I haven't treated you fairly, I know."

Must she hit him over the head before he understood?

"It's more than that. You refuse to share your feelings. You distrust me. Why?"

"I've made several mistakes. All I know is, I want you in my life," Darius admitted, his voice almost a whisper.

He almost looks ashamed to admit it Moriah thought. That's not good enough, her subconscious scolded she would maintain her stance. There were several unanswered questions. She would make him open up.

"I need some time," she replied softly.

"You will consider it?"

"I don't know why I should. You are self-sufficient, you don't need me."

"But I do."

"You can hire a housekeeper, Darius." Her voiced edged with painful remembrance.

"To hell with a housekeeper. I want a wife." Darius regretted his choice of words.

"Oh, I see. You want to expand the job description?" she remarked sarcastically. Moriah noticed a muscle twitched along his cheek and the stubborn set of his jaw.

"I don't grovel. If that's what you want, then.." He stood and walked toward the door. He paused after opening the door, Darius said over his shoulder, "Give it some thought." The door closed quietly behind him.

He acted as though he hadn't heard a word she said. Moriah was furious but she had the good sense to hold her tongue. Darius was the most infuriating man she had ever met. Talking to him was useless.

Agitated, Darius drove home as though a thousand demons chased him. He handled the situation poorly. Somehow the words got switched around somewhere between his brain and his mouth. Darius had guarded his emotions so long, he found it difficult to convey his feelings for her. Great! A trip to Austin for nothing," he said aloud. He'd taken the first step, now it was up to Moriah.

Tonight sleep did not come easily to Darius.

~* * * *~

Over the next week Darius threw himself into breeding the new bull and doing repairs around the ranch. He never mentioned Moriah's name again. Jason sensed the subject was taboo and stopped asking. Darius tried to push her from his thoughts but she continued to fill them both day and night. He wanted Moriah in his bed not for lustful reasons. He loved the scent of sweet jasmine on his pillow when he woke with her each morning.

Jason commented that Darius grew short tempered more each day, just the same he did not take the hint. Instead his pride took over and he refused to chase after her. If she wanted him, she knew where to find him.

Moriah began her job as interpreter for a large investment company. At the end of the first week, her boss summoned her to his office complimenting her performance. A sense of well-being and accomplishment filled her. This called for a small celebration she thought riding the bus home that night. Pizza was far from nutritious but this was a special night.

After unlocking the door of the townhouse she sat her briefcase and purse on the hall credenza. Inside a large vase of red roses greeted her. A card peeked from between the leaves. Curiosity filled her as she moved toward them. How did the flowers get into the townhouse? Who sent them? The card read:

Moriah, the roses are red however they pale next to your beauty. Please come home. I don't want to live without you. Love, Darius

Moriah was astonished. This was the first time she had laughed in days. The note was corny but she cherished it nevertheless. This was out of character for Darius. Maybe there was hope? Grasping a tender bud between her fingers, Moriah leaned to inhale its fragrance. Elation filled her. She would not be easily swayed Moriah considered, she must be certain of her decision.

~* * * *~

Lamar searched *The Flying M Ranch* for almost an hour. After stopping the truck's engine, he climbed out and sauntered in Darius's direction.

"Hello, Lamar." Darius removed his hat and wiped the sweat from his brows. "What brings you out this way?"

"Tonight is the raffle," Lamar began. "I wanted to stop by to remind you."

Darius was being polite in asking he told himself. "What time's the raffle?"

"Seven." Lamar sensed Darius's tension. "How have you been?"

"I'm fine. Did Nora tell you what happened?"

Lamar nodded. He knew how Darius felt. He almost lost Nora and everything that was important to him because of his insecurity years ago. "Yes, Darius. I'm sorry to hear that."

Darius shrugged as if it were of little consequence. "It's not bad. I manage to stay busy."

"Nora tells me y'all been separated for a month now. It will do you good to get out -- to see people. Will you come?"

He appreciated Lamar's sincerity. Darius smiled. "I wouldn't miss it for the world."

"Okay. See you then." Lamar turned and started for his truck.

~* * * *~

CHAPTER 18

Nora called Moriah on Friday afternoon. "C'mon, it'll be fun," Nora coaxed. "Besides it will give us a chance to visit."

"I would like to go, but I'm tired."

"You're not stressing yourself?" Nora inquired. "Are you seeing the doctor regularly?"

"In answer to both questions, yes." Moriah laughed. "I mean, no I am not stressing myself." Nora made a sound of disbelief over the wire. She acted like a mother hen Moriah thought. "How is your family? How's Megan?"

"She's healing nicely. Thanks for asking," Nora replied. "Once Megan was feeling better, Lamar took me away for a week -- it was wonderful, just the two of us. He said we needed the time alone. We left the kids with a close friend."

A sick feeling washed over Moriah. She resented her friend's happiness. Just hearing about it brought back painful memories. Darius offered to take her away for a honeymoon. In any event she wanted to teach him a lesson. Truth was, there was more to it. What troubled Moriah was her insecurity as his wife.

He neglected to tell her he loved her, he only mentioned he wanted a son.

"Moriah?"

She mentally jerked herself to the present. "Uh, yes?"

"Are you sure you won't change your mind about coming?" Nora prodded. "Darius will be there," she baited.

"No!"

"There's no need to raise your voice." Nora held the receiver away from her ear.

"I'm sorry. I cannot right now."

"It won't be as much fun without you," Nora continued. "Sorry but I have to go."

"Thanks for calling." Moriah hung up.

~* * * *~

Later that evening Darius met Lamar and Nora at the school. He hadn't realized how starved he was for human contact -- he arrived thirty minutes early. Darius understood the Women's Club planned a potluck tonight followed by a bingo game. The drawing for the truck would be the finale.

"We're glad you could make it tonight," Lamar greeted.

"Thanks. I appreciate that." Darius slapped Lamar's back.

"How about some brew?"

"You bet."

Lamar strode toward the keg of beer. "Bring me one to," Nora called after him. Her husband halted and glanced over his shoulder and nodded in acknowledgment. Nora and Darius took seats away from the crowd.

When they were alone, Nora said, "Have you contacted Moriah?"

Darius answered her with a question of his own. "Didn't she tell you?"

Nora shook her head.

"I see."

"What will you do?"

"It's her move."

"I take it you have contacted her? She's being stubborn?" Nora knew it was not her business but she couldn't resist.

"Apparently she does not want me."

"How can you say this?"

"It's true. I tried to make amends for my mistakes." Darius gave a low snort, a disgusted expression fixed on his face. "It's over."

The potluck dinner and bingo game helped to fill the horrible void Darius felt. It would take a long time before Darius recovered from his relationship with Moriah. But he vowed he would. Nora and Lamar tried their best to cheer him. Outwardly he smiled and laughed, whereas inwardly he experienced an ache that refused to go away.

Each day for the next two weeks, Moriah received a dozen red roses with a poetic verse scrawled on a card. Each touched her heart more than the one before. Still he hadn't called. Other than the roses she might have thought he'd given up. Moriah was grateful Darius had not. She was determined he would fight for her, or she didn't want him -- roses or otherwise.

At least the nausea subsided Moriah considered as she dressed for work that day. She was steadily gaining weight now. Already she appeared as if she had a basketball beneath her clothes. Out of desperation yesterday she went shopping because her clothing no longer fit.

Depressed, Moriah favored oral gratification -- eating although she was not hungry. Each day she rushed to the mailbox hoping to find a note from Darius, only to leave disappointed. Even the roses had stopped. She thought she had him right where she wanted him, that shortly victory was in hand. Sadly Moriah discovered she was mistaken. Her glimmer of hope was extinguished.

Evidently Darius meant what he had said. Moriah was well rid of him! She was grateful she hadn't mentioned the child. Her suspicions about him proved correct.

Why hadn't she remained in Malaysia?

Because she wanted a better life. Had she remained there she would not have this life growing inside her now. She struggled to focus her thoughts on the child. Moriah hoped the child looked like Darius. She loved him more than life itself. A one way street left one open to abuse, she reminded herself. One of life's little jests Moriah thought disdainfully. She steeled herself against the tears that threatened to fall.

Nora called once a week to check on her and to keep her abreast of the local gossip. She never mentioned Darius and Moriah wondered why. Soon summer became fall and Moriah entered her fourth month of pregnancy. Her job was wonderful. Waiting for the arrival of her child she thought everything was perfect. She busied herself with decorating the nursery in yellows and greens and began to buy baby furniture as expenses allowed.

A few of the men she worked with that vied for Moriah's attentions ceased all efforts once they learned she was pregnant. The most important thing to Moriah was having this baby. She would give it all the love she'd been unable to give Darius.

November arrived and Moriah began Lamaze classes. She was six months along still she hadn't told Darius. She was growing accustomed to the idea of being a single parent. This child was the center of her universe. She arranged time off work to have the baby and to recuperate before returning to work. The telephone calls from Nora dropped to once a month now. Moriah didn't begrudge Nora her life. She understood that her friend had three children and a husband to care for and a life of her own.

~* * * *~

"How's it going, brother?" Carrie greeted when Darius answered the phone.

Silence prevailed.

"I'm glad you're doing well," she chuckled. "Mom tells me you are separated from Moriah?"

"That's hardly a news flash. It's been three and half months now."

"The way I hear it, Moriah's going to have a baby," Carrie said casually. "She has no plans of telling you. Just thought you would like to know."

His jaw dropped somewhere around his ankles. "Are you sure about this?"

"Why would she keep this from you?" Carrie enjoyed Darius's turmoil - this was what he needed to spur him onward, she considered. Carrie felt she owed him after meddling in his life -- she only meant to help.

He was dumbfounded.

"Darius?"

His confusion and hurt were replaced by anger. "You're sure about this?"

"Why would I lie? I owe you one, brother."

If Darius hadn't been shocked to hear about the child, he might have enjoyed having Carrie make amends. "Where did you hear this?"

"Nora."

"We're even, Carrie." Darius cut the connection. He telephoned Nora and reluctantly she confirmed Carrie's story. He felt like a raving madman. Moriah knew she carried his child and deliberately set out to hurt him. He was entitled to the child and regardless of the situation, he would rise to meet the occasion.

The thought of a son brought renewed fight in him. If necessary he would take the child from her. How could anyone be so vindictive? He could deal with the fact she didn't want him. But he would not leave the child, regardless. Darius telephoned his lawyer to learn his options.

First of all he must do nothing to disturb Moriah the lawyer informed him, at least until the child was born. But that was three months away! In addition there was the chance she could leave the area without a trace. He could not risk losing the child, he would play it her way, for the present.

Darius paced as he tried to formulate a plan. She mustn't become suspicious of his motive for staying in contact with her. Maybe he would hire a detective to follow her? Then he could stay abreast of her activities without being a threat. Darius decided he would be so damn sweet, she wouldn't know what to think. Lifting the telephone, he punched out the number. Anxiously Darius twisted the cord between this thumb and forefinger, waiting.

He could tell from the sound of her voice she was genuinely surprised to hear his voice.

"I can't believe it's you, Darius." Her voice was husky with emotion. Why had he called? Moriah had lost all hope of any reconciliation between them.

"How are you?" Darius asked casually.

"Fine. And you?"

"Moriah, I want to apologize for oh, so many things. I've missed you. When I didn't hear from you, I assumed you didn't want me in your life."

"Why did you call?"

"When I was not served with divorce papers, I hoped. I thought," he voice faltered. "Tell me if, I'm wrong. Do you think there's a chance we could try again?" Darius held his breath. He had never wanted anything more. He hadn't realized until his anger abated that he used the child to hold onto Moriah.

"You don't want to pressure me, right?"

Hell, it sounded good to him! Darius jumped to the excuse. "Correct."

"That's unbelievable," Moriah exclaimed. "You respected my wishes."

Darius learned when her voice softened in this manner she was warming to him.

"I learn slowly, but I'm trying," he said in his most endearing voice. Darius knew he was a stinker, but this was an unusual circumstance.

Enjoying the conversation, Moriah clutched the phone tighter. "I trust you look better than the last time I saw you?"

"What?"

"Are you sleeping better at night?"

"Oh, that! You mean the dark circles?" Moriah drove him mad when she laughed this way. It reminded him of the times they were locked in the throes of passion. Does she realize she has a soft, sensuous voice? He wondered. A shiver ran up his spine. "You'll be relieved to know, they're gone." Darius tried to sound equally at ease.

"I really appreciated the roses, Moriah added. She felt terrible that she'd never called to thank him.

"Aw!" Darius dismissed them as inconsequential. Hell, he was syrupy at the moment. He wasn't sure what possessed him to do this.

"And the notes?"

What roses? What notes? Darius wondered. Then it occurred to him – Carrie! No wonder she said she owed him one. She'd messed with his life and he didn't even know it. He disliked the thought of asking her for help. The roses were her idea. But if he supposedly sent the flowers with Carrie's help, what the heck he considered. He remained silent.

"You must think me callous?" Moriah hazarded.

"What makes you say that?"

"It has been three months since you sent the roses, and I never called to thank you," Moriah pointed out.

"Not necessarily."

"At the time, I thought you were greasing me up," Moriah defended.

He laughed. "I did ... what?" It felt good to laugh again he thought.

"You know, what I mean ... butter, yes, butter me up," Moriah said in exasperation. "Darius you made me lose my concentration." She paused to collect her thoughts. "I thought you wanted to make fast work of having your way," she supplied.

"I will admit. I dislike the word no."

"You sound like you have changed the leaf," Moriah said with enthusiasm. "How do you say it?" When she was nervous, Moriah had difficulty with American idioms.

He laughed a hearty baritone sound. "Turned a new leaf."

"That is, what I mean."

"I have realized my mistakes. A man's pride can get in the way and tie him in knots." His voice softened seductively.

"You wrote the sweetest notes," Moriah reminisced. He remained silent.

"I could never pass as a poet," Darius added.

"What was it you wished to tell me?"

"I prefer to say it in person."

"What is wrong with the telephone?" Moriah hoped he would not insist on seeing her. She couldn't bear the thought, she might break into tears.

"I find it hard to say over the phone. I hope you understand?"

She groaned silently in despair.

"What if I come by, can we discuss it?" Darius coaxed.

Moriah feigned ignorance. "Hm?"

On a lighter note, he began, "We could discuss it over hot chocolate or coffee. C'mon!"

The words escaped her as if by their own volition. "Yes. That would be nice."

"Great." His voice reflected his eagerness. "When can I come by?"

"What's wrong with, now?" Her heart fluttered with anticipation.

"I need a shower. I will leave in --"

"You can shower here." Moriah was convinced she'd taken leave of her senses.

"It's a deal." He hung up. Darius grabbed his overnight bag, threw some clothes inside and was on the road in minutes.

Forty minutes later he was knocking on her door. Moriah swung the door open and his jaw fell.

After closing the door, she patted her stomach. "I know what you must be thinking."

"Right now, my brain's not functioning." He dropped onto the sofa.

"I will get the chocolate."

Did she have anything stronger he wondered? He knew she was pregnant, but he was not prepared for the size of her. She looked like an overripe piece of fruit, Darius thought. Her hair and complexion were even more radiant and beautiful than he remembered. He struggled to gain his composure. When he saw her minutes ago, it was as though someone slammed a fist into his stomach. After a few slow, deep breaths, Darius felt much better.

She returned with the steaming liquid at last and set the cups on the small table.

"Why didn't you tell me?" Darius asked biting back an angry retort.

"As you say, some things are difficult to say over the phone," Moriah hedged.

"Well?" He sipped the drink not because he wanted it, but to keep his hands busy.

"You go first," she said adamantly.

Darius cast her a puzzled look and he took another sip of the warm liquid. He worked to mollify the anger and hurt he repressed. He knew Moriah did not respond well to anger; she would clam up. He had to much at stake to risk losing her. Tentatively he cleared his throat.

"Okay." Impatiently he ploughed a hand through his hair. "I've always had trouble with words." He would choose them carefully. "I have been self-centered and stubborn," he began. "I vowed, I would never allow a woman to manipulate me."

"Who hurt you, Darius? Nancy?"

Slowly he inclined his head."We were both head-strong. I travelled a lot in pursuit of my career. Once when I returned from an assignment, I found her in bed with a close friend of mine."

"So you built a wall around yourself and decided women were not to be trusted?"

He whispered, "Yes."

Now, his behavior made sense.

"Not all women are like Nancy. You over compensated for her betrayal by building a shell around yourself," Moriah managed. "Darius, you never gave me a chance. You never gave us a chance."

Darius was relieved to have it out in the open. "I chose a mail order bride, you," he said, "to stay in control of my life. I did not want to share my private life with anyone." Darius gazed deeply into her eyes. "That's no longer the case."

"In what way do you mean?" She refused to let him off the hook easily. He must say it Moriah's heart cried!

"I'm lonely as hell without you. I told myself in the beginning, I wanted a wife in order to have a child, a son. When actually I wanted a mate but wouldn't, or couldn't admit it even to myself."

"You were afraid?"

"I don't have all the answers. I want you in my life, if you'll have me?" Strangely enough, he meant it.

Moriah's unanswered questions caused her to hesitate. "You can be obstinate at times," she said considering. "I would insist we freely communicate our feelings to one another."

Moriah searched his face for a response.

"You once said you loved me. Did you mean it?" He carefully assessed her reaction.

"Yes."

"Tell me, again." He moved closer to her on the sofa. When she did not draw back, Darius took this as a green light. His eyes implored her as he repeated the question. "Tell me?"

"I love you, Darius." The words barely escaped her lips when his head dipped.

The kiss was feral and filled with passionate longing. He was like a thirsty man in the desert who finally stumbled onto an oasis. He drank of her sweetness.

"Oh, Moriah. I've been a fool." He trailed kisses along the curve of her neck. Her enlarged breasts pressed against his cheek. "I need you."

"Darius?" She was drowning with desire.

With hooded eyes he gazed at her. "Yes?"

"Maybe you should take that shower now?" Her eyes were clouded with love and other emotions he would try to decipher later.

He understood the message her eyes sent. "I won't be long," he said, lifting his overnight bag.

"Promise?"

Darius shot her a wolfish grin. "I promise."

When he went the wrong way down the corridor, she intervened. "It's the third door on the left." He paused for a moment, turned and entered the correct doorway.

~* * * *~

CHAPTER 19

Twenty minutes later after a shower, Darius joined Moriah in bed. The sheet barely covered her breasts he noticed. His chest swelled with pride.

"Are you sure this okay?" he asked.

"If you still want me?"

"I have never wanted anything more," He dropped the towel from his waist and slid between the sheets.

"C'mere!" Darius invited. Moriah giggled as he reached for her.

"Uh-oh!" she exclaimed. "We have a problem." Her gaze shifted to her abdomen.

"I see what you mean." He pushed up on his elbow and leaned to lightly brush her lips with his. For a moment Darius brought his hand to cup her cheek, then he let it trail lightly along her breasts to rest on her abdomen in a stroking motion.

He lifted his eyes to hers. They were filled with passion and something else she couldn't make out. Moriah wondered if he loved her.

"Ever heard of side saddle?" he whispered huskily.

"Show me."

Gently he drew her to him taking great care with his movements. Darius kissed Moriah long and hard. Lovemaking was a little awkward Darius thought but it was good to have her in his arms once more. He almost lost Moriah. This he could not bear.

His sensibilities heightened and his body trembled under her touch. She was the woman he had yearned for. Somehow he'd known from the beginning but refused to admit it.

Moriah thought he couldn't possibly find her appealing. She couldn't blame him, she was huge. Each touch of his hand was a slow, gentle caress. His tenderness hadn't surprised Moriah. She suspected all along that once he lowered his defenses and allowed himself to be vulnerable, he could be sensitive and caring. And he was.

Darius caressed her femininity, arousing Moriah to new heights. Their lovemaking was slow, gentle and different this time. It held all the tenderness of a rose petal, Moriah considered as they climaxed. He rolled onto his back afterward his lips forming an "o" he blew out an exaggerated puff of air from his lungs. This warmed Moriah's heart.

He stroked her abdomen as though it was the greatest treasure in the world.

"What was it you wanted to tell me earlier?" she persisted. Moriah regretted breaking the spell except that he deserved to know the truth. Her hand moved to her abdomen as she spoke. "Darius, I am sorry I kept this from you."

"Why did you?" he asked softly.

"I thought you wanted a son, not me," Moriah confessed.

"How could you ever think that after the times we made love?"

"You spoke only of the child. And you were distant. What could I think? I was not confused that you lusted for my body."

He gave a seductive grin as he appraised her. "Well maybe a little. After all its not a bad one," Darius teased. Her look of disapproval pleased him.

Darius's expression became serious. "I tried to protect myself by holding you at distance," he explained. "There's something I haven't told you."

"After we split, I learned Nancy was pregnant with my child."

"How could you know for sure?"

"She was pregnant before I left for an assignment. She wanted me to give up my career. I told her if she loved me, she would understand and not ask me to make the choice. We fought terribly before I left. We said some terrible things. She must have despised me. She planned to tell John the child was his. I learned much later she lost the baby." Grimacing, he paused. "When I confronted her with this, she told me she had never wanted the child."

His eyes flickered momentarily with remembered pain as they sought Moriah's. She moved her arms to embrace herself about the waist. "I'm not Nancy. I want this baby." She paused to collect her thoughts.

"You forgot one thing."

"Pray tell?"

"Do you love me, Darius?"

"I thought you knew."

Moriah shook her head. "Tell me?"

"Of course, I love you," Darius whispered huskily.

"How long have you known?" Moriah asked.

"Since the trip to Arkansas. I realized I couldn't live without you that it must be love. It hurts to much," Darius admitted. "I've loved you from the start I suspect."

"You're just saying that," she taunted.

"No. You frightened the hell out of me. I've never loved a woman in the same way. You came into my life disrupting everything." Darius mouth spread in a broad grin.

"Do you really mean it?" Moriah ventured. He nodded. Smiling she said, "Trust me?"

His grin belied his serious intent. "Should I?"

"You can count on it." The words no sooner escaped her, Darius leaned and took her mouth in a feral kiss.

"Does this mean you'll come home?"

"I can think of no place I prefer more."

~* * * *~

"Darius, you remembered I love roses!" Moriah exclaimed as a man brought a vase into the hospital room. She could barely take her eyes off her husband holding their son.

With the sound, he lifted his head from the tiny bundle in his arms. "What?"

"The roses, you remembered," Moriah repeated.

He looked confused for a moment then said, "Well, yes." Darius's face colored.

"I told him you liked roses," Carrie interrupted.

"You didn't?"

Carrie extended her arms much as a conductor would. "I'm afraid so."

Moriah's eyes shifted to her husband.

178

"Yes, but I am the one who sent the roses," Darius pointed out.

"And the notes?"

Carrie shrugged. "Well, one out of two isn't bad, Moriah. You see I have this brother who is about as poetic as dirty laundry. I figured I'd better help him or heaven knows what might have happened." She shook her head. "I shudder to think."

"Okay Carrie helped me with the notes," Darius confessed. Why couldn't she be happy knowing he made the effort? "When that didn't work, I --"

"What?" Moriah demanded mockingly.

"I worried a lot."

Carrie and Darius exchanged an anxious look.

"She told me you were pregnant," Darius supplied.

"Would you have followed me if, I were not with child?"

"Settle down," Darius encouraged softly. "Yes, sooner or later. Carrie knew how I felt about you. She helped me forget my fears and set aside my pride to go after you."

"You're right. This is history," Moriah conceded. "What's important now is our son."

Carrie moved alongside Darius, gazing at the newest member of the family. "He's beautiful. Chris and ... what's his name anyway?" Carrie paused to shift her gaze to Moriah.

"His name is Darius Chadwick Mc Coy," Moriah remarked proudly.

"The kid will hate you for it." Carrie teased. She resumed her hovered position over the baby in Darius's arms.

"Hello, Chad," she greeted, lifting a small hand that curled instinctively around her fingertip. "Look! Already he's crazy about women. Chad and Chris look more like brothers than cousins. Don't you think?"

Moriah nodded in agreement.

"He's wrinkled, how can you tell?" Darius questioned in a teasing tone.

Carrie rolled her eyes at him. "Men! You give them a sweet package and they complain. Come away with me kid, I'll treat you right."

"Over my dead body," Darius enunciated each word clearly.

The door to Moriah's room suddenly swung open. Rebecca and Seth Mc Coy hurried inside. Rebecca wasted no time gathering Chad in her arms. She began to make sounds only a doting grandmother would make.

"Hello, everyone," Seth greeted. "You'll have to forgive Becky. She never thought Darius would have children." He moved to Moriah's bedside, embracing her. "That's for a job well done," Seth chuckled.

"Thank you. I had help."

"I see you're feeling fit," Seth added.

"Oh Seth, isn't he wonderful?" Rebecca said summoning her husband to her side. "He looks just like Darius when he was a baby." Seth considered her comment for a moment. "It hasn't been that long ago. You remember?" Seth nodded, cradling his wife's shoulders with one arm.

Carrie crossed over to where Darius stood beside his wife. "Someone you know called me the other night?" she taunted.

"What? I mean who?" Darius asked curiously.

"He said he was a good friend of yours."

"Darius knew Carrie's reference was to Ben. "What else did he say?"

"He said he wants to see me. Ben said you would approve," Carrie said playfully. "Are you a matchmaker now?"

"Who? Me?" Darius shot Carrie an innocent look.

"Did you agree to see Ben?" Moriah prodded.

"If you must know, yes. He plans to visit me in Arizona," Carrie confessed with a more than pleased expression on her face. "He claims he's thinking of relocating to Arizona." Shifting her eyes to Darius, Carrie said, "Imagine that."

"I'm sure it's coincidental," Darius remarked casually.

Somehow, Moriah doubted his innocence.

~ THE END ~

ABOUT THE AUTHOR

Melisant Scott is an aficionada of the romance genre. She has enjoyed reading romance novels for several years, alas she decided to try her hand at writing. She hopes everyone enjoys reading, A Mattter Of Convenience, a story about a mail order bride. Melisant's hobbies include sailing, music, classic movies, her cats and her home is Texas.

Other books to look for by Melisant Scott are *Paradise Caribbean Style* and *Reluctant Heart*. To purchase your copy of others books by Melisant Scott on the internet visit: *Open Window Publications*. Most of her romance books are available in both paperback and digital (e-books) formats. Be sure to follow Melisant Scott on *Facebook* or *Twitter*. Watch for the release of her next book, *Forbidden Passion*.

Resources: facebook.com/scottmelisant ; twitter.com/melisantscott ; openwindowpublications.com ; melisantscott.org ; amazon.com/author/MelisantScott

www.ingramcontent.com/pod-product-compliance
Lightning Source LLC
Chambersburg PA
CBHW071247210626
46818CB00013B/438